Best Friends

When Friendships Go Beyond Boundaries

TRACY L. JONES

ISBN 978-1-950818-83-9 (paperback)
ISBN 978-1-950818-84-6 (ebook)

Rushmore Press LLC
1 888 733 9607
www.rushmorepress.com

Printed in the United States of America

CONTENTS

Chapter 1: Three the Hard Way.................................5
Chapter 2: Those School Daze!..............................14
Chapter 3: Can We Say Goodbye? 23
Chapter 4: On the Greens...................................38
Chapter 5: Meet the Martins 58
Chapter 6: The First Date?.................................87
Chapter 7: Where's the Party? 96
Chapter 8: Friends or Foe 120
Chapter 9: How Can You Spell Relief?..................146
Chapter 10: And the Bomb Drops!.......................176

Epilogue..185

CHAPTER 1

Three the Hard Way

<u>Veronica</u>

Okay I packed my outfits, my shoes to match every outfit for both evening and night. Now I just need my make-up, personal products, hats (it's very hot in Houston) bras, panties, extra sexy panties for those just in case late nights and my hair supplies. Ok that should be about it Veronica thought. I hope I didn't forget anything. If so hopefully I'll remember it before I leave. She took one long look around her room. She couldn't believe how much junk she had lying around everywhere. There's no way she could clean all of this up before Lawrence gets there. Oh well it will just have to do for now.

Veronica was so excited to finally be attending her fist golf tournament with her dad and in Houston, Texas. He always wanted her to go with him the past but she was always too busy. This time she promised her dad that she would make time to attend with him no matter what. She went shopping as early as two months ago, that's how excited she was about this trip.

Not only was she just happy to be going with her dad but she finally gets a chance to meet her favorite golfer Warren Beasley. It would be nice if he was as fine in person as he was on television. He is one of the finest men she has seen in a long time so she knows for a fact that a lot women are going to be all in his face. Most of them are surely only going to be there to see him. They may not even know a thing about golf but she bet they know plenty about him. She knew she had to look incredibly enticing to get his attention. I want to look so fine she thought that his eyes wouldn't be on anyone else but me.

Where in the world is my ride? Lawrence knew he was due to be here a whole hour and half ago. When it comes to me going anywhere he takes his sweet time Veronica stated trying not to get irritated. She looked out the window to see if she finally seen his car. Just as she thought he was nowhere in sight.

If he didn't own half of the company I would fire his behind. She hoped nothing goes wrong next week that would cut her vacation short. The last time she went out of town five employees quit. Three of them were women he dated then dumped. They somehow ended up finding out about one another. What they end up doing to his BMW was not pretty. The other two just decided to leave because they no longer wanted to deal with the drama. I've told him several times in the past that you can't date a woman and at the same time sign her pay check. Does he listen to me? Nope! I'm tired of coming home cleaning up his mess.

His stuff better be together this time or he will have some serious problems out of me.

The only real regret I have about going on this vacation is that my mother and sister is coming along. For some strange reason my dad felt as if this had to be a family vacation. Lord, of all people he could've invited to tag along why did it have to be them? I know they're family, but a whole week with them is asking me a bit much. He claims our family has been distant for the past two years so he wanted us to spend some quality time together.

Honestly two years away from them wasn't even long enough if you ask me. I could go another two, maybe even four without seeing them. Heck, why not go even further and say a lifetime, believe me it would be worth it.

I already know how this weekend is going to turn out. My mom will spend half of her time trying to mingle with celebrities and putting me down for not being my sister Valerie. Of course, my sister the Diva Val will spend her weekend flirting with every man there and thinking every woman is jealous of her because she's a supermodel (who cares).

My dad without failing will spend his time defending my mom for saying something stupid, putting my sister in her place, taking up for me, and wishing he never planned the whole vacation in the first place.

I love my sister but I can't stand her at the same time. She's the type of person that acts as if everyone is beneath her. She is constantly trying to tell me how to act and how to talk around people.

There's never anything or no one that's good enough for her. That's exactly why she doesn't have a man. What man in his right mind would want to date someone like that? Someone who's controlling, vindictive and always must have things her way. He would have to be rich, stupid, and patient.

Valerie has been my mother's favorite since we were kids. All my life I would hear "Why can't you be more like your sister Valerie?" "Why aren't your boyfriends as nice as Valerie's?" "Why don't you have as many popular friends a Val?" Why don't you have this like Val, why didn't I have that like her. I mean the world didn't revolve around her precious Valerie.

I guess me owning my own clothing business weren't good enough for her Val. She often stated that selling and designing clothing for a living was meaningless. Like wearing them for living and walking back forth for other people like me for a living was better. When it comes down to it, I stand to make more money than she ever will. I think she really needs to get her priorities straight.

Like when the first met Lawrence. My mom and sister couldn't stop drooling over him. Valerie kept talking about how fine he was. She often asked me how in the world did I end up with a friend that fine. What did I really have to do to get his attention. That was in no way none of their business. I wasn't about to tell them how we met for them to talk down about me even more. I knew he was fine but I thought since we both had a past there was no way he would dare date Valerie. Wrong!

They for sure dated thanks to my mom. She did everything she could to get them together. Whenever he came over to visit she would make sure they both ended up around each other. Even striking up conversation for them asking questions like "Lawrence isn't my daughter gorgeous? She's single you know. Isn't he fine Valerie? You have a girlfriend baby?" It took everything in the world to keep from strangling her.

When we would have dinner Lawrence and I usually sit beside each other so we could laugh and crack jokes. She would go as far as making me to get up and would sit my sister beside him at the table. That was my mom's way of making sure they got better acquainted. Now you know I won't having that. Enough was enough!

She always made it her priority to get her princess a date but when it came to me she could've cared less. Mom wanted so bad for Lawrence and Valerie to be together she would send them out on dates, and even made sure she paid all expenses for their prom. She was so bad she would even spy on them when they went out on dates just to make sure he didn't look at other women. I know a pure nut case.

All my mother's melding finally paid off they finally went from just dating to going together. That was all I could stand. The last thing I wanted was to see them together even if it meant killing her and that wasn't too far behind. I mean I was really hurt by the whole ordeal but did anyone consider my feelings?

So, you know my next move was to break them apart. My mom said I was just acting out because I was jealous of my sister and her new boyfriend. The nerve of her, he was my friend first. Like I said before they didn't even consider the past I had with him not even him. I was just as pissed with him than I was with her. The only difference was I still liked him so it didn't stop us from remaining friends.

When I finally told our other best friend Chasity what was going on she wasn't happy about it either. She said I had better do something and fast or she would. Knowing her past we really didn't want that to happen. So, we got together and schemed up a plan. I talked Chasity into posing as Lawrence's ex-girlfriend when they went out on a romantic date.

Chasity was good she really made a scene. She made it seem like Lawrence had dated her, had sex with her and pushed her aside. I asked her did Lawrence say anything. She said no. He just stood there throughout the whole ordeal because he thought she had lost her mind.

The next day he called and cussed her out so bad it wasn't even funny. Then he cussed me out because he said he was sure the whole idea was mine. Yeah whatever like Chasity doesn't have a dark side.

Valerie was heated with him after that. She didn't speak to him for a whole week. So, our prank almost worked um yeah if Chasity and Val didn't meet at a party a week later. Dammit momma! Believe me it was a huge disaster, way too much to explain. Just take my word for it.

My mom suggested that someday that they could end up getting married. Has she lost her mind? That would be over their dead bodies! Of course, that meant she would have to kill me first because there was no way that was happening. I was nob longer in love with him but I be dog gone if I was going to allow him to marry my sister.

Now my mother Debra is everything my sister Valerie is and everything I'm not. She's very judgmental, and manipulative but likes to disguise it as being a concerned mother (yeah right). She's the type of woman who must do everything by the book. She was a college grad with a Doctrine in psychology. They say most psychiatrist needs to be evaluated just as much as they evaluate you. That has been nothing but true over the years.

You can't do or say anything out of the ordinary around her. You must have perfect posture, diction, grammar, and always dress a certain way when she's around. Her favorite saying was "You must always keep yourself presentable you never know who could be watching you. So, you have always present yourself as if you always had it all together." Whatever that supposed to mean.

She could also at times be a mean and hateful woman and always wanted things her way. Growing up I had it hard. Instead of going outside to play she would make me stay in the house because she thought I was too tomboyish. She said I needed to stop playing in dirt and started wearing more dresses and heels.

Who in the world wanted to wear a dress at the age of ten? I sure in the heck didn't. I wanted to wear my shorts, tees so I could play with my friends and climb trees. You know that made her angry with me.

Now Val on the other hand was the complete opposite she was the type that loved wearing dressing. I guess that's why she turned out to be a model and I didn't. I was very rebellious and argumentative with my mom from then on whenever she asked me to do anything. I think she hated me from then on. I always thought she was crazy. After that, whenever she'll ask me to do something and I said no she would lash out in a rage for no reason.

My dad had to check her into a mental hospital one year ago, because she threatened to kill him. They never told us exactly what it was about, all my dad said mom had been under a lot of stress lately. I'm not sure how true that was but I never questioned it any further. I went home to visit to help dad out for a little while. We didn't get the chance to see each other while she was in there. That was the best two weeks of my life. While I was home my dad kept getting a lot of strange phone calls. Someone would call and hang up. Every time I asked him about it he reacted as if he had no idea what I was referring to.

They finally let my mom out. I can't say that she was so called cured but she was more pleasant to be around. Dad said that she swore to never do that again. Her story made front page in our town and all her friends was talking about it on Facebook. She couldn't imagine having people talking about her behind her back. Val called home when she heard about it panicking having a fit. She told everyone to make sure we kept her name out of all interviews. That heffa has always been selfish.

Now my dad Richard on the other hand, you couldn't tell he was related to my sister and married to my mother. People often thought I was a female version of him. We often mirrored each other's personalities very well. We both was were hard working, kindhearted, and driven. I was blessed with my mother's beautiful hour glass shape and curvy hips but my sister was blessed with my dad's tall, handsome, lengthy statue.

He was a fair skinned very handsome fifty-nine-year athletic man. He was still flirted with by women of all ages even at his age because of how young he looked and the way he always carried himself. He was also a well-known business man and a self-made millionaire. He was the first black man in his city to own and operate a company selling golf equipment and golf apparel. He also was the first man in his family to have a both a Masters in Technology and Doctrine in Business Science.

Everyone that knows him would say that he is straightforward, kind spirited, giving, but can sometimes be what we both are too easy. He sometimes let too much go instead of dealing with it, that made him seem like the weaker person. That was mostly true when it came to my mom. He was always allowing that nut get on his last nerves. I think he spoils her entirely way too much. Everything she asks for she gets, everything she says must always be right.

My mom and sister has always been jealous of our relationship. Why shouldn't he spoil me? My daddy loves me I'm his baby, right? Wrong at least in my mother's eyes. She swears he let me get away with murder. Which means she's going to keep a close eye on me this week making sure I don't do anything to embarrass her.

Yes, this is going to be a wonderful vacation. If only all of us weren't going. Ok, now where in the world is Lawrence? He is now an hour and a half late! He really gets on my nerves. He thinks he can do whatever it is he wants to do. Not one time did I inform him that he can get here whenever he gets ready. He knows I run a tight schedule.

I don't have the time nor the patience to deal with him today. So, he better make for darn sure he's on his way. Let me at least try to call him again. I don't know why he has a cell phone, he never answers it. Oh well.

Oh, yeah, I know there was something I was forgetting important my toothbrush. I wouldn't dare forget that. I better put it in my makeup bag that way for sure I won't forget it. While I'm waiting for Lawrence I need to be calling Chasity to remind her that I'm leaving today.

"You have reached the phone of Chasity. I'm sorry I'm not available at this time. Please leave your name number and a brief message I'll promise to get back with you at my earliest convenience."

"Chaz! Where are you girl? You told me that you were staying home today. Oh well, I'm leaving whenever Lawrence slow behind arrives. So, when you get this message hit me up. Alright hunni talk to ya later."

That's strange she wasn't home all day today or yesterday. She usually doesn't go anywhere without telling me where she was going. Mmm, I'll get that straight with her later. Ok now Lawrence should've been here or called by now. If he's not here in a five minute I'm calling to fuss him out.

Now who is this call me? "Hello?"

"What's up. I called to tell you that I'm on my way."

"Where in the world are you? You know I'm running late!"

"I know, I know baby, I got tied up at the office. Everything is alright now."

"Excuse me? First, if there was a problem at the office you should've called me and informed me of the problem, secondly, what did you mean by now?"

"It was nothing really. Naomi just forgot to deposit the money again and turn off the alarm system. I took care of it so you don't have to worry."

Is he insane Veronica wanted to scream! Not worry about our money being messed up? Is he kidding me? "Well it was enough for you to go way down there and take care of it yourself. I knew she was going to be irresponsible when I first laid eyes on her."

"Well I'm part owner of this business and I think she's doing an excellent job. What's a little mix-up?"

"I see her huge breasts have literally caused you to lose your mind. If she has another mix-up like that we'll be filing for bankruptcy!"

"I'm surprised at you Ronica, you should know me better than that, Lawrence responded a little irate. You know I would never hire someone unless I thought they were well qualified for the job."

"Okay so please explain to me after all the mix-ups she has caused why is she still there?"

"I'll find out when we go out for dinner tonight," he added laughing.

"What in the hell do you call that?"

"Being well qualified for the job if you ask me."

"That is not funny Lawrence, besides you know that is no longer allowed. What will happen if you two don't hit it off, where would that leave us?"

"Hopefully things will go very, very well."

"You know if you keep thinking with your privates they're going to get you into some serious trouble."

"Why should care it didn't get me anywhere with you?"

"Why are you even bringing that up? That was a long time ago"

"See you don't want to talk about that."

"Anyway, enough about that, where are you?"

"If you look outside your window you're see my truck parked out front in your lot."

Sure, enough when she looked out the window there he was sitting outside in his truck. I wonder how has that idiot's been sitting out there before he said anything she thought? Knowing him, he may have been out there the entire time. She yelled down for him to come up and help her carry her bags to the truck.

Instantly she ran to the bathroom to check her makeup and to make sure that her hair and clothes were straight. Hold up! What am I doing? Lawrence is not my man. When did I start caring about how he thinks I look?

He's fine and all but in no way, am I doing all of that for him not ever again. Besides the way, he views women I don't think my face will be the first thing he notices anyway.

When he gets up here I'm sure his arrogance will most likely start to get the best of me right off the back. I know some men can really be sure of themselves but he takes it to the extreme. I would rather not go back down that road again with him not this point in my life. He will not take my mind off meeting that fine Warren Beasley this weekend. I can't hardly wait!

CHAPTER 2

Those School Daze!

The sound of Lawrence ringing the doorbell broke Veronica's concentration. She took one last look in the mirror put on some lip gloss and ran downstairs to open the door. When Veronica looked up she saw a 6'4 handsome walnut complexioned brotha standing at her doorway with a sly smile on his face.

He was wearing a black fitted blazer, dark wash jeans, a silk plaid shirt and Italian made shoes. He has a beautiful muscular physic to compliment his silhouette. His body looked so well defined in those jeans it was as if it was chiseled out of stone.

Lawrence always had the most gorgeous set of calves and thighs Veronica has ever seen. In the summer, he made women weak when he wore shorts. He use to walk around on the court flexing his muscles trying to get all their attention. That was not hard to do because brotha was fine. Just to see him without his shirt on alone would drive even a blind woman insane.

He had the most beautiful set of dark brown eyes that could mesmerize you just with one stare alone. When he talks directly to you he has a way of making you think that you were the only important person in the room.

His lips oh lord, was so juicy they would put L. L's to shame. She often enjoyed watching him speak just to see them move back and forth.

Yes, when they made this man they broke the mold. There weren't too many men like him around anymore both fine and successful. He was a good catch and he walked around like he knew it. Just seeing him took her back to their college days when they all first met.

*   *   *

I was madly in love with Lawrence in college to the point I could barely live without him she explained. It took God and a lot of prayer to break my depression I had over this man.

He was the type of man you didn't have the strength to say no to nor the courage to leave alone. I see I still have that problem to this day. He knows exactly how to get to me when it comes to getting something he wants. He would stop at nothing until he gets it no matter what.

He has been the same exact way since college. That's how we met at Maryland State University. I can't say that Lawrence and I has always been best friends. As a matter of fact, we weren't even close at all.

Lawrence, Chasity and I have been friends since my sophomore year. I met Lawrence my freshman year. I was known as a wall flower/nerd on campus. I was considered a pretty girl I guess but at the time I didn't like to wear makeup nor dress up. I just wasn't that much into clothes at that time. I was really excited about finally being on my own away from my parents and into the college life. That was until I laid eyes on this tall, lengthy, dark skinned boy with the prettiest set of white teeth walking into the computer lab room. Later that day our professor assigned us to be lab partners for a thesis. That was a huge part of our final grade.

Lawrence was the star basketball player that year. That made me feel extra special that I was picked to spend time with him. I found out later that I was asked to be with him because I had the highest grade in the class. He never really had to work hard for anything it was pretty much given to him. His grades often reflected that. They wanted him to get with someone that would help him get a high grade on his final. That meant that I ended up doing most of the work but he took all the credit for the A+ we received.

Everyone was so crazy about him especially the women professors. He practically got away with murder. I felt special that was spending so much time with him. He would sometimes cancel his dates and times out with his boys just to spend that time with me. I know it was only because of the project but I use to pretend it was only for me.

We were spending so much time a lone that I started falling in love with him. I found myself wanting to be around him constantly. I would follow him around campus, I would call his phone and leave him text messages asking him what time he was coming over. I didn't want anything I just wanted to make sure I was always available.

I made sure at that time that no one and nothing kept me busy. I had to keep telling myself that it was only for a grade to keep from losing it when he didn't return my calls.

Some nights he would stop to get something to eat or I would cook on nights we didn't have much money. I mean it felt like a real relationship. At least for that one month he made me feel special. I was so in love that didn't think that one day it could all be over. For some stupid reason, I thought we were starting to be close friends.

I was far off. After the project was over I completely stopped hearing from him. No phone calls, visits nothing. After all he no longer needed me he had his grade, right? I remembered I had his number. I would call to see if he wanted to go grab something to eat or go to the movies. He wouldn't answer like before, it would now go straight to voice mail, I would leave a message. Of course, he never returned them.

On some days, he would pass by me in the courts with his frat brothers I would wave he just purposely ignored me. You would think that would stop me but no I kept perusing him.

One semester I took a side job in the office to keep from going home filing papers. I ran across his files and found out his birthday was coming up. So, like a dummy I wanted to do something special to surprise him. I ordered flowers, balloons, and a huge teddy bear with candy and had them sent to his last class. I really wanted him to feel special, I wanted so bad to see his face when he received it. I didn't enclose my name because I just knew he already knew it was from me.

Days had passed, I hadn't received a thank you phone call, text or nothing. I assumed once again he knew I was the one that sent it. I know I had to be an imbecile to think that spending time together doing a project could turn into a relationship but he had my mind all over the place.

As popular as he was I should've known better. A couple of days later I saw him walking in the hallway. I was nervous but decided to approach him anyway.

"Hi Lawrence haven't seen you in a while, how have you been? Veronica asked nervously.

"Fine," he answered a little annoyed.

I was a bit disturbed from the look his face but I decided to keep talking. "So, did you get the gift I sent to your class on your birthday?

He smirked looked her up and down the said "Oh that was you." Then simply walked away.

Veronica just stood there frozen not sure what to say or do next. She should've said something anything to him to keep him from getting away with embarrassing her like that. Instead she stood there in embarrassment with a stupid look on her face. She could've died right there and not even had cared. People around her were starting to whisper and saying little things she knew were about her. By that time, she was passed devastation and felt low. She felt her feet moving fast with hot tears rolling down her face. She had no idea where she was going but at the time she didn't care long as it was far away from where he was. She spent the remainder of her afternoon crying in the library. That's how she met Chasity.

She was walking by when she overheard someone crying in the corner. She really appreciated Chasity because she was the only one that cared enough to stop and give her a hand that day. Everyone else just kept walking, I guess they didn't want to get involved.

"Hello are you ok?" Chasity asked.

That was all Veronica heard at that moment. She was so weak she could barely talk.

"I know you don't know me but would you like to talk about it?"

"Thanks, but I'll be fine", was all Veronica final managed to get out of her mouth. She was helped to her feet as she tried to get herself together. She finally explained to Chasity what happened and what she did to set herself up for it.

Chasity understood but stated that no man was worth all that drama no matter how fine they were. She said that she was far too important to allow some man to bring her to that state of mind.

Come to find out Lawrence was a childhood friend of hers. They both grew up in the same hometown. She stated that she only come to that school because he was there. At the time, Veronica thought that was strange but then again, didn't think nothing of it.

She said that Lawrence had always treated women like they weren't his equal. He felt as if most women had no brains and that they were good for only one thing and that's giving pleasure. He never really been in a serious relationship so he had no idea how to treat women. Like that was hard to believe.

I've found out that she was the only woman that he never mistreated at all. That's because he knew she wouldn't allow it. She was known to be a very strong willed and confident woman. I knew she wasn't the type of woman that would take any mess from a man like him. I've noticed that he did respect her as well because when he came he treated her different. He knew what to say and what not to say. I often wondered over the years why he respected her so much she thought?

After that day in the library those two were always together. When you saw one you saw the other. Of course, when Lawrence seen them together he didn't know how to react. He instantly caught a terrible attitude about it. He couldn't stand seeing them two together. He often made it his business to keep them apart.

She thought he secretly had a crush on Chasity or something strange had went on between those two; the way he was always carrying on. Chasity was a beautiful dark complexioned woman with the looks of a super model and a shape of a vixen. Whenever they would go out to a club or a bar men would practically throws themselves at her feet.

He was no exception. He drove me crazy acting stupid when other guys tried to talk to her. Later I even tried to copy the way she acted and her style of dressing to get his attention. That was even impossible because she was so unique.

Far as I know she never looked at him as nothing but a friend over the years even though I know he wanted more. She wouldn't dare want to date someone as arrogant and childish as he was. I pray he later dismissed it all as just a childhood fantasy and moved on.

We were all around each other constantly. First it was hard for Veronica thought but over time it began to be easier and easier. It was less tense somedays and more intense on others.

Chasity felt like she was always in the center of it all trying to help them two keep the peace. That never seemed to last long. The tempers between the two of them would flare up so bad, sometimes she would just walk away and leave them both standing there arguing up a storm.

That's pretty much how things were in the beginning. Lawrence and I just simply hated each other that was until I came back to school from summer break. Lawrence was still the man on campus but I was longer considered the wall flower he was used to seeing. You can say I matured quite a bit over the summer Veronica thought.

Veronica no longer wore the long floppy dresses. They were not now form fitted and showed off her shapely figure. She now wore make up and regularly kept her hair done. She even went as far as wearing the latest fashion and designing her own clothing.

She was even getting a lot of stares from cute and popular guys on campus, even Lawrence. That was weird for her because she wasn't used to receiving that kind of attention. Lawrence no longer treated her like the third wheel. He was even trying to holla at a sista!

Like an idiot without hesitation she gave in. She didn't even try to put up a fight. She just wanted to prove to herself that with the help of her new looks that she could get him. You know how most female's minds work; we have to make it seem like finally getting him was effortless. Knowing inside we're trying to do whatever it takes to get you.

We dated off and on for a while but nothing I would consider serious. I wasn't about to give my body up that easily. No way was Lawrence about to have his cake and eat it too. She made sure he knew she only went out with him when she wanted to and not a moment sooner. Shoot I'm not stupid I know he was the same one that dogged me just a year earlier.

He managed to still maintain a messed-up attitude, that made it hard for us to stay together. Even though he was trifling that wasn't the breaking point. One night we were in my room studying for our midterms. I was trying to stay focused but he had his mind on something else.

All night he spent most of his time kissing me on my neck and blowing in my ear. Whenever I pushed away he would try his best to move down below my waste. He constantly tried putting his hands down my panties to feel on my most personal parts. The more I tried to keep him away the worst he got.

I know he should've been in my room but I thought it was just going to be just an innocent study session. After all we were there to only study, right? Wrong! At least that's what I thought at the time. My mind was on one thing and it was very clear that his mind was on helping me lose my virginity.

He kept staring into my eyes and trying to kiss my lips harder than he was looking at his books. I would pretend like I was concentrating on what I was looking at more than him hoping that would defer his focus elsewhere. I didn't want him to know that I wanted him more than he wanted me but I know I had to keep it together. It was getting harder and harder to resist Lawrence by the minute, I did find him extremely sexy. I found myself staring at his lips and the definition of his muscles made the in the room climb ten more degrees.

About twenty minutes had passed and then he was at it again. Each time his force became stronger and stronger. Of course, I kept playing hard to get. There was no way I was about to fall for that trap for him to have my name destroyed all over campus.

We studied I know until well after two thirty in the morning, well I studied and Lawrence begged. He asked could he spend the night since it was too late to go back to his dorm. I said it was fine, but he had to sleep at then opposite end of the bed (big mistake). I fell asleep at the top of my bed thinking that he was going to keep his end of the bargain.

Every now and again I would feel his foot touching my butt trying to get my attention. I would ignore him and pretend like I was asleep just so he could leave me alone. It worked for a while.

About another hour had passed when she felt him inching his way to the top of the bed. Before she could open her eyes, she could now feel his breathe on the back of the neck. She thought for a moment before she slowly started to turn while contemplating if this really what she wanted. She could feel his body inching closer and closer to her face. She didn't dare stop him because she was interested to see just how far this was going to go.

Every part of her was getting very nervous now. She never thought it would get this far. Yes, she was still a virgin and all her life her dad made sure she kept it that way. If he could see her now, boy what would he say. He always told her that what she had was a gift. Heck just his threats alone made anybody want to keep their legs closed.

The next thing she knew their lips were touching. Lawrence, had he sweetest tasting softest lips she ever tasted, but she felt nothing. There was no fire, no sparks, nothing. She never had sex before but she knew it wasn't supposed to feel like that. He started to rub his hands over her thighs. That got her a little excited but that was about it. Then she felt his hands slip into her panties that made her nervous. He started rubbing and kissing her harder and harder, but again nothing. Nothing at all. She was wet down there but clearly that was about it. By that time, she thinks Lawrence felt it too because he suddenly backed away. He just had this weird blank look on his face. She didn't know what to tell him. Veronica just realized that she didn't have feelings for him in that way at least not sexually. From that point they knew that they were meant to be no more than just friends.

It's was a chance that Lawrence may have been hurt from it but she would've wanted it happened that way than for them to make the biggest mistake of their lives. He left the room that morning with one of the most disappointing looks on his face. He hasn't spoken of it since that day.

After that they decided that they're friendship meant more to each other than a one night stand. She explained to Lawrence that she wanted her first sexual experience to be with the one she loves or at least was in love with. Not someone she had no true feelings for. He claimed he understood but knowing Lawrence it's possible all of that went in one ear and out the other.

When she mentioned it to Chasity the next day she had an attitude. Veronica wasn't quite sure if was towards her or Lawrence. She dismissed it as nothing at the time. She was sure that it will come back to surface one day, and when it does she was going to have lots of questions.

CHAPTER 3

Can We Say Goodbye?

"Hi" smiled Lawrence as he walked through the doorway.

"Hi yourself", Veronica responded.

"Are you finished packing yet?"

"Now that was a crazy, question. I have been finished packing since nine o'clock!"

"Oh."

"Oh?"

Lawrence walked in looked around the room like he usually does. He frowned his face when he saw the mess that Veronica had laid out all over the bed. She really didn't care about the faces he made about her mess he knew she wasn't a clean freak. He unusually bypassed the mess sat down on the couch with this weird look on his face as if he was thinking about something.

That was strange for him because he was always out spoken and always said exactly what was on his mind. He picked up the remote and started surfing channels. Veronica was puzzled by his quietness but she dared not ask what was on his mind afraid he just might tell her.

"Why are you sitting? You know we have to put the bags in the car."

"They can wait."

"Look I don't have time for your nonsense. I really have to get going. So, get off your behind and help me put my bags in the car!"

Lawrence walked pass her as if she hadn't said a word and started looking out the window. She just continued packing her bags, no way was she about to allow him to get into her head. She had no idea what was wrong and wasn't even sure if she even wanted to know. All the sudden out of the blue she heard a loud sigh.

"Are you ok?" she asked puzzled.

"I don't want you to go, I want you to stay here with me. I need you."

Veronica laughed to herself. Is he serious? I can't believe that just came from his mouth. He was the last person she wanted to hear say something that stupid like "I need you". Man please. What did he mean by he needs me? He never said that to me before.

At first she thought he was joking but he had this sincere look on his face that made her think something different. In the past, he only said something silly like that when he didn't want her to go anywhere. How did she know this wasn't another trick of his? Then she gave him a second glance. He never once blinked nor cracked a smile. I guess he really must be serious she questioned?

"You are serious? What would make something like that come out of your mouth?"

"Ronica you'll be gone for a whole week and I won't have anyone to talk to."

"You've known that I was going to Texas for two months, and never said a word until now. Why?"

"I knew if I said anything before now you would still go."

"What make you think that now I would change my mind?" Besides don't you have a date with that huge breasted Naomi Thomas? Remember her? Veronica asked.

"Oh, I see you got jokes huh?"

"Yes, I do, and so do you."

"Naomi means nothing to me. I don't love her like I love you."

Love! Did that negro just say love? I knew something was seriously wrong with him but this right here takes the cake. I'm going to ignore the fact he just said that. "What about Chaz? she should be here."

"Chaz will still be out of town."

"She will? Where is, she going?"

Lawrence got up to look at himself in the mirror his favorite thing. She saw that he was purposely trying to ignore her question. Something strange was up she could feel it.

"Does it have to be this weekend?"

"First, you need to stop it. You already know this is my family's only time we will have to get together. Rather or not I want to see my sister or mom I'm not disappointing my dad for anyone."

"Your dad's not the only reason that you're going."

"You're right I'm defiantly going to see Warren Beasley."

"So you're telling me that you would rather be there with him than here with me?"

Immediately Veronica turned to face Lawrence trying her best not to laugh hysterically in his face. "Why would I miss an opportunity to see him just to stay home with you?"

Lawrence raised his eyebrow as if he was carefully trying to anticipate his next response. "What does he have that I don't have?"

Way too easy Veronica laughed.

"Besides, Lawrence replied clearly now upset, you only like him because he's a millionaire."

"Grab a bag."

"Why are you ignoring my question?"

She kept putting her final accessories in her bag without saying a word. Honestly if he wanted to know his question wasn't worth answering.

"I think you're ignoring me because it's true."

"No, I'm ignoring you because your statement was totally untrue."

"Ok, then you answer me this. Why do you happen to like Warren so much?"

Veronica stopped packing trying to keep her nerves under control. She knew that Lawrence was trying to accuse her of something stupid something that she surely was not. He thinks all women are gold diggers unless you are giving up something then he views that as payment like most of those chicken heads he dates. So, it'll be a waste of time trying to explain anything to him.

"Well I'm waiting for my response?", Lawrence implied.

"Truthfully I only like the way he plays golf." Veronica knew she was lying through her teeth but there was no way she was about to make him aware of that.

"I'll meet you downstairs, Lawrence replied laughing hysterically.

"What's so funny?"

"I'll be outside," he yelled this time laughing even louder.

He gets on my last nerve, but she had to laugh to herself. She knew for a fact that everything that she just said about Warren was a lie. She could care less about him being a millionaire, there was nothing that he could buy her that she couldn't buy herself. So, Lawrence should know he was far off with that.

It was his looks and the way that he carried himself that attracted her to him. He was a very distinguished and well-dressed man. A quality she found most attractive. He even looks good in his clothes on the greens she could only imagine how he would look with them off the greens. His walk was unbelievable. Just that alone always got her attention.

Watching him play while walking back and forth was enough to always get her warm. She loved the way he would tune everything out around him to prepare for his next shot. It takes a special person to have that type of concentration.

Then it was the fact that he was a business owner and very active in his community as well as many other things that makes him stand out. The man has looks and brains who can ask for anything more.

Veronica walked towards the window. She stood there watching Lawrence struggle trying to put her bags in the truck. He looked stupid dragging her bags back and forth. Serves him right for laughing at her.

"You want me to get the other bags or do you, have it?"

"Are you done laughing?"

"Veronica you're a trip."

"What?"

"You don't think I know you were lying through your teeth?"

"What do you mean?"

"I mean I know what type of woman you are and I know what type of men you are attracted to. You say you're not interested in Warren for his money I'll give you that I know you have your own. I do know for a fact that you have a fit every time his name is even mentioned."

"Your point is?"

"My point is that you are crazy for that man and it has nothing to do with the way he plays golf."

"Well, yeah so what if I am?"

"Well you know how men like that treat women like you," he stated once again checking himself out in the mirror. He is so dog-gone conceited!

"Hold up! Excuse me? What do you mean men like that treating women like me? They treat us like what now? Will you stay out of the damn mirror!"

"Anyway. I'm just saying men like us find women like you easy."

"What!" Has this man lost his mind? I have heard him talk crazy in the past but he has clearly taken it way too far this time. I should slap him silly for that silly comment.

"I can tell by your expression that you didn't get where I was coming from."

"You had better explain yourself and your answer better be a good one."

"I'm just saying it's hard for men not to take women like you for granted"

"Okay there you go once again. What in the hell do you mean by women like me?"

"Veronica you're a beautiful woman that owns her own business, you're a good woman that don't drink, don't go out to clubs, to top it off you're a virgin. Men see women like you as fresh meat really. He's an athlete. He has his choice of any woman in the world sometimes many at one time. On top of that he's a pretty boy. You're not used to that type of life style. He would have your noise open before you know it."

"Just like you did?"

"I'm just saying you're a good woman and that you deserve better than that"

"Well, thanks but I'm a big girl and I can take care of me. I don't think I would deliberately allow someone to mistreat me. Besides I probably won't even see him"

"Oh, you will. I know you. You won't stop until you try everything in power to get him to notice you."

"What would make you say something like that about me?"

"I know how you can be. You're do anything to get attention."

"Personally, I don't like that type of attention."

"Since when," he asked folding his arms across his chest.

"What's that look for? I'm not some type of groupie that chases celebrities around trying to get their attention."

"Really? What about that time we were in college and we went to that Genuine concert and you followed him back to his hotel room. Then you and Chasity had the nerve to camp outside his door waiting for him to come out?"

"That was a long time ago. Besides he later dropped the charges," Veronica added laughing.

"Yeah, yeah whatever. I never understood what you saw in men like that."

"You didn't seem to have a problem with it in the past when I was chasing after you. On top off that what about Naomi?"

"Veronica I told you Naomi means nothing to me, you know that."

"That's the problem I know she means nothing to you, but you keep leading her on like she does. You and I both know that you could care less about her but it still doesn't mean won't expect her to give it up tonight."

Lawrence didn't have much to say because he knew Veronica was telling the truth. Reading his expression, you could tell he wanted to respond but he knew if he did and the wrong thing come out it would spark a whole new argument. "I'm just saying watch yourself that's all."

"Lawrence Weldon are jealous?"

He walked away ignoring the question. That was okay he didn't have to she already received her answer. How in the world could he still possibly be in love with me? That was so long ago. So much time had passed. She had dated guys he has dated many, many females since then. I honestly thought his feels had subsided by now. I guess I was wrong.

Still he was always quick to judge, but when it's thrown back at him he doesn't know how to take it. Even Naomi with her huge breasts deserves more than that. The feelings I have for Warren is only a little crush. It's not like I'm going to ask him to marry me. He's always making a big deal out of nothing. This is my vacation and I'm going to enjoy it and him every chance I get.

Who knows if I'm lucky I could end up spending half of it with Warren. Anything is better than spending a whole week cooped up in my mom and sister's face.

I think Lawrence is really pissed off at me, he won't even look my way. He'll be alright just as long as he put those last two bags in the trunk I could care less about the attitude.

Now all I have left to do is take one more look over my apartment and make sure that everything is in place. My neighbor Sarah said that she would keep an eye on the place for me, checking the mail making sure I don't get robbed!

I will lock the door and that will be it. Could Warren be how Lawrence said he could be? I guess time will tell. That's everything. Oh, no my cell can't be ringing now. Who in the world can this be? Veronica checked her phone and it was her mom's cell number.

Shoot she thought. I should let it go straight to voice mail then she would think I was on the plane. No, suppose it's dad. I really wouldn't mind talking to him. I just pray that when I answer this phone that it's him not her on the other end. Well here goes nothing.

*　　*　　*

"Hello?"

"Why are you still home?", her mom asked yelling in her ear.

Something told me not to answer that phone. I should hang up right in her ear. "Hi mom."

"Don't hi mom me. Do you know your father and I have been here in Texas going crazy thinking because we were running late you were here waiting? Get here and you're nowhere to be found."

"No I did not," Veronica responded sarcastically.

"Veronica Martin I could do without your sarcasm. When are, you leaving?"

"My flight leaves in thirty minutes."

"I hope you'll be on it."

"Mom it's not my fault I'm running late my ride just got here. Veronica looked around the room trying to find something to focus on to distract her attention away from her conversation. Her mom was starting to piss her off already. The one time she needed Lawrence to walk through the door he didn't. What was he doing outside anyway?

"Don't you own your own car?"

"Yes, but I decided to leave it home. I asked Lawrence to drive me to the airport."

"I don't want to hear your excuses. If your ride wasn't there on time, then you should've called a cab or asked Chasity."

Look you old witch! She wanted to shout through the phone. "Mom it's no big deal, Chasity is out of town anyways. Besides I'm taking the next flight out."

"That means that you will be here around three o'clock. That will be way too late," she snapped.

"Too late for what?"

"Your sister maybe too tired to socialize after her long trip from Paris."

"What about me? Won't I also be tired?"

"I don't see how. Your flight's not that long?"

Veronica let out a big sigh into the receiver. Something told me not to answer this phone she contemplated. "Look mom I'm already running late, I really don't feel like getting into this with you before I leave."

"I was just being concerned that's all," she snapped

"I know you were. Where's dad?"

"Look Veronica! I'm not going to allow you to ruin our family vacation with that snobby attitude."

"All I did was asked where was dad? Is it a crime to ask about him now?" She felt her voice rising, that meant the conversation was starting to get out of hand as always. Just then Lawrence finally walked in the room and not a moment too soon. He instantly knew something was wrong from the expression on her face.

"Your mom?"

"Who else"

"Oh."

"Hello are you still their child?"

"Yes mom, I'm still here."

"Well here's your father, it's obvious you no longer want to talk to me."

"Sure don't," Veronica murmured.

"What was that? Look young lady I" …

"Hi Peaches", Richard chimed in on the other end of the phone.

"Daddy! I'm so glad you finally took the phone away from her."

"I know baby girl, she's mad at me now. Look at her rolling her eyes he added laughing. I felt the tension heating up between the two of you so I took the phone."

"Let her stay mad, good enough for her."

"Peaches, you know she's still your mother, she deserves the same respect you give me."

"I know, I know dad. She just makes it so hard."

"You still need to try. Ok why are you running late?"

"Dad you know how slow Lawrence can be. Besides I've already told your wife that I was taking the next flight out."

"Okay I understand, just hurry up and get here. I miss seeing your face. It's been awhile. Your mom misses you too, she just has her own way of showing it."

"Really? I can't tell. I didn't mrean to spend as much time away from you but it's just that I can't stand being around her."

"I know baby," Richard agreed a little bothered.

"Is her favorite there yet?"

"No not yet. Her plane should land shortly."

"Then why is she running her mouth at me and Valerie's not even there yet?"

"I guess she wanted to make sure you were still coming."

"Why so she could put me down and complain the entire time?"

"Humph." was all she heard from the other end of the phone. For a second she noticed that she was starting to sound just like her mom. She did nothing but complain from the time her dad got on the phone. He hears enough of that from her already daily, to hear it from her she knew it could be too much right now. She knows she needs to apologize but her mom just knew how to push the wrong button sometimes.

"Hello?"

"Yeah baby girl I'm still here."

"I apologize dad. I didn't mean to take all my frustration out on you. Mom just knows how to push the wrong button sometimes."

"It's okay. Well let me get off this phone. I love you and I'll see you when you get here okay."

"I love you too daddy."

"Have a safe flight. Give Lawrence my love."

"I will."

"Okay good-bye now."

"Bye daddy."

I think I hurt my daddy's feelings. "Sniff." I'm sorry daddy, I didn't mean too, your wife just really gets under my skin. I've found lately I'm starting to talk to people the exact same way that she talks to me. Something must give. There is no way I'm turning into that woman. I guess I do carry her awful traits. He needs to divorce her is what he needs to do, that way she'll finally be out of the picture.

I don't know why I still allow my mom to get on my last nerve. She has always known what button to push to make me upset. How could someone be so mean and heartless at the same time? Is she happy Veronica thought?

Anyway, this is not the time to be sitting here thinking about my mother and her ways. I have a plane to catch. It's bad enough that I must spend a whole week with her. Maybe I should take a flight someplace else and just get lost. I would have to blame someone for it. Why not her?

She looked out the window to see where Lawrence has gotten to. It has been a few minutes since he's been upstairs. She knew he had to be up to no good, he was too quiet. Oh! No wonder he's talking to Lauren Krauss the biggest flirt in the building. I can't stand her. The only time anyone sees her is when a man is somewhere around.

Look at her. Everything he's saying is not that funny. I hate the way she throws her hair back when she laughs, just sicken. I should embarrass him I'm ready to go. I don't have time for him to be social-izing. He can talk to her later.

"Lawrence! Are you ready to go yet?" she yelled.

They both turned and looked up at her. Lawrence had this weird look on his face. "I'm ready whenever you are", he responded.

"I'll be right down." No, she didn't just look at me and roll her eyes, crazy heffa. He don't want nothing on you but one thing. Believe me it's certainly not your phone number.

Veronica took one last look around grabbed her makeup and headed out the door. Lauren walked away when she saw Veronica walking out the door. She walked passed without so much as a hello. "Yeah you better walk away before you regret it."

"You can be a trip sometimes."

"Whatever."

"You didn't have to embarrass me like that."

"Yes, I did. You know I'm already running behind and you're out here talking to her like you have nothing else to do."

"Why is it when you're talking to someone you're not in a hurry but when it comes to me you're running behind?" he asked

"Just come on, we can discuss that in the truck."

"So, what did your mom want?"

"She was talking about nothing as usual, trying to get on my last nerves like always."

"Same ole, same ole huh?"

"Pretty much. So, what you and Miss thang was talking about?"

"None of your business noisy."

"Well excuse me." Veronica ignored his comment reached over and turned the radio on. She was trying to drown out his attitude with the sounds. She looked over at him he had that normal nonchalant look on his face.

"Don't even try to act like that. You know I was just kidding."

"It doesn't matter if you tell me or not. I'm sure it probably was about much of nothing."

"How you figure that?" Lawrence asked now a little disappointed.

"I know you Lawrence. Knowing you it was about getting some booty later."

"I'm hurt. That's all you think I'm about?"

She paused and then gave him a weird look. She tried her hardest not to come right out and say "Hell yes, I think you're a superficial pig!" Quickly she decided to lie her way out of it. Knowing that the truth would hurt his feelings. "No, I don't think that way about you at all. You're actually a good man but sometimes you can be misleading." Lord knows I must repent for that lie! Please forgive me.

"Really?"

"What now"

"I mean, really. Why did you just sit there and lie to me right to my face? Woman I've been around you long enough to know when you're lying through your teeth. I'm disappointed that you of all people only sees me that way."

"Well to be honest Lawrence it's not my fault. It's pretty much your own doing. I'm sorry to say but you're not the type of man that leaves a lot to the imagination."

"Meaning."

"Meaning a decent woman with common sense would know what you wanted as soon as you approached her regardless how fine you were."

"That's not always true. There were plenty of times I've approached women in my gym clothes and didn't receive that type of response."

"Mmm hmm. Later how did that date end?"

"How did you know it was a date?"

"How did it end?"

"I'm saying I didn't ask for things to turn out the way it did."

"Case closed!"

"You really didn't make a case because that's not saying a thing. Women can sometimes be misleading themselves."

"That can sometimes be true, but we only respond to whatever vibes men are giving us. If those vibes are negative from the beginning that's what we give back. Say for instance when you approach a female and the first thing you do is hit on her. Say she's the type of female that likes that type of approach, of course you would expect to get some on the first date."

"That may not always be the case as well. There were plenty of times I have met women and didn't do anything on the first date."

"Ok, I don't believe that, but I'll take your word for it."

"Well let's say you skip this trip and we go on our own private vacation. You're looking really hot in that outfit today you know that", he added with a wink.

"See what I mean," Veronica yelled hitting him hard on the shoulder.

"What?"

"What my behind. You can't even go a second without thinking about sex."

"What, you're afraid of what big daddy might do to ya?"

"Man, you need help."

"You know you want me, why don't you go ahead and admit it."

"You're full of it you know that."

He slowly mouthed the words "I love you". Watching his lips move made her temperature go up a few degrees. There was no way this man could still get her warm she tried to convince herself, but he could.

"It is getting warm in here. What is the air on?" Look at him with the smug look on his face. "Why are you looking at me like that?"

"Why you think?" Lawrence responded slyly.

"Anyway, I'm sorry I even asked."

"Yeah right."

"Changing this subject have you heard from Chasity?"

"You don't have to change the subject. I can always go with you and we can share a room with no problem."

"Lawrence, would you please stop acting like that and answer my question?"

"Yeah, she called me this morning, he added laughing. She stated that she was attending some seminar in Miami FL. She said she was having a nice time being around other doctors. Not sure what that supposed to mean."

"Oh really. I see she failed to tell me that she was going any-where. So, did she say how long she will be down there?"

"I think she said a week. You two should be back around about the same time. I thought you knew that?"

"Nope, I haven't heard from her since last week."

"That's strange. I thought you two talked about everything."

"So, did I."

"Veronica had no choice but to wonder what has been up with Chasity lately. For the past couple of weeks, she's been acting kind of weird. She has acted distant in the past but she has always remained in contact with them both. Not once had she gone out of town and not told her where she was going. Something serious could be wrong this time though. I just don't understand this is not like her. It has now been a whole week since I've talked to my best friend. I'll find out what the problem is when I talk to her later. There better be a good reason why she's not talking to me or she will regret it.

Lawrence pulled up to the curb at the airport. He helped Veronica with her bags, gave her long hug and a kiss like she was going away forever. "Ok let go! I'm not going off to war."

"You might. I feel like I'm letting my baby go."

"Let go of me with your silly self."

Lawrence gave Veronica on last hug then he was on his way. He asked her to bring him a souvenir back, something expensive. He always wants something expensive but won't contribute any money to help pay for it. I may fool him this time and bring him back something cheap. After about fifteen minutes she saw her flight flash across the screen "Now Boarding for Texas gate 201 A." Well here goes nothing. Lord please be with me on this plane ride and help me endure this week.

CHAPTER 4

On the Greens

"Excuse me madam may I take your bags for you?" asked the handsome bellboy.

"Yes," Veronica added with a smile.

"Okay madam your suite will be located on the seventh floor room 778, stated the manager behind the counter. If you have any additional questions you can press the red button on your phone in your room. Someone will be available for you."

"No, I don't have any questions right now. I'm just ready to get to my room."

"Very well then, Here's the keys to your suite. Your insurance should cover them if lost or stolen. Now I just need your signature," he stated pointing to the black dotted lines on the electronic pad.

"Sure," Veronica stated trying not to sound frustrated. Does he have to be so pushy she questioned. Why is he asking her so many questions? I'm tired and ready to take a shower. Can't we take care of all this mess later?

"Thank you so much. Okay madam that should be it. The young gentleman will help you with your bags. Enjoy your stay and welcome to the Lady Victorian," the manager finally ended with a smile.

Finally, she thought! "Thanks, you too."

Veronica turned to take a good look around the hotel. The place was absolutely breath taking. Her dad had made reservation down town at the Lady Victorian hotel. The building was huge and beautiful. It was white and shaped like a palace. The building was located right in the middle of everywhere. He made sure they didn't have to drive to get to anything unless they really wanted to.

The building was beautifully lit with handmade chandeliers hanging from every corner of the high ceilings. The inside of the building decor color scheme was of lovely colors of crimson reds, beiges, and cremes scattered throughout the room. The furniture was also modern yet Victorian with an elegant rugs to match.

There was a circular staircase in the center of the room facing the door draped with red carpet flowing from each side. There were huge oval shaped windows that also complimented the room and gave the room a romantic feel. The floors where made up of shiny red and gold marble tiles that were elegantly placed in an oval pattern creating a captivating scene as if you were walking on melting gold. Yes the place was breathe taking, it was almost looked like a scene from my favorite old movie as a child.

The common area was busy today. Maybe it was due to the tournament going on that weekend. Veronica never seen so many people together like this without a lot of mess going on. I guess growing up in a small town you're get used to seeing anything. She wasn't from the hood but going to stay with her cousins when she was younger she was exposed to some very interesting things.

She looked around to see if she could spot Warren anywhere. Could he be staying in this hotel she thought. Nah he couldn't be. There's no way they would allow him to stay there. That would be too obvious and he would get way too much attention. It would be nice if he did though, he would be only five minutes away for the club. She wouldn't mind running into him in the mornings coming out of the elevator.

Veronica was thinking that it would be nice if Warren came there alone. I don't know how I would feel if I ran into him with a female on his arm. I wouldn't be able to flirt like I wanted to she thought. He better be by himself or else. That may sound crazy but I want him to myself, so what if I don't want to share.

They finally reached suite 778. When Veronica walked in her room her mouth almost hit the floor. For the first time, she was speechless. Her room was absolutely breathe taking. Her dad out done himself, she doesn't remember the last time seeing anything that beautiful.

The décor was the same as commons area except there were more cremes and beige as the accent colors. There were two rooms adjacent to each other on the right located off the large living room with queen size beds. The rooms also came with their own separate bathrooms and walk-in showers. One even came with a red jacuzzi! There was a full kitchen with a stocked fridge and a huge picture window overlooking the city.

She hadn't counted on the room being that beautiful. Her dad made it almost impossible to leave. She didn't know if she wanted to spend her vacation with the family or in her suite. As hot as it was outside she may end up spending most of the daylight inside.

"Where would like your bags ma'am?", asked the bell boy.

"In the first bedroom on the right will be fine, thanks."

Wow look at this view! You can see the entire city from here. When I finally buy my home, I want a view just like this one. My dad did an awesome job once again I must say. I don't think I've could've done better.

You know my parents forgot to mention where they were staying. Lord, please say it's not with me. It's bad enough I don't want to spend a week being around my mom so there's no way I'm sharing a room with her for a whole week!

Oh, lord my phone is ringing again and I just got here. This time I'm not even going to answer it. With my luck, it would be my mother again screaming in my ear "Where are you now? Why aren't you here, why aren't you there?" I'm not in the mood for that right now. I just want to take my shower, change my clothes, and pray I make it to at least the end of today's round of golf.

"Okay ma'am I put your bags away. Is there anything else you need before I leave?" I'm not sure if that's what they usually supposed to ask because he was grinning just a little too hard.

"Um no, thank you, but I'm fine. Here's your tip." Veronica reached into her purse and tipped him a twenty.

"Wow thank you ma'am you have a nice day."

"Thanks, you too." The bellboy was cute and built she thought but he was way too young. I could get my Stella on and try to holla at him anyway. I'm sure won't anyone know but him and me? Nah with my luck he would have a big mouth and tell all his buddies that work in the building. I would be humiliated, my name would be ruined, my mom would find out and surely disown me, then my dad would find out and kill him. Nope not even worth his young life. Besides I don't want to be known as the slightly older woman that seduced a young bellboy.

I would rock his world so good he wouldn't have no choice but to tell all his friends. Let me stop, who am I kidding. Who really feels like babysitting she laughed.

What should I wear today? Something sexy or something casual? Hmm. What about my tan romper shorts with the arms out? That would be appropriate for any occasion. It's casual yet sexy. It's sleeveless but tasteful enough to not be too much. I could add my tan and white straw hat to top it off. It feels like it's at least a hundred degrees outside. I need to wear something to keep cool.

Veronica couldn't help but continue to be puzzled about the Chasity situation. She had yet to hear from her and the day was almost gone. She knew her cell phone number so that was not the excuse. Then again maybe she should just leave things alone all together. The way she has been pushing her away lately she's not even sure if she should waste her time reaching out to her. She's not even sure if she wanted to hear from now at all.

They haven't gone that long without talking in the past. Even in they argued they always apologized most of the time the same day. It has been a week now and nothing. She's not even sure what to think.

If she had done something to her then the silence and the distance would make a lot of sense but that is not the case. Veronica wants so bad to be angry but what kind of friend would she be if something was seriously wrong?

Then again suppose nothing is wrong and she's just acting her normal stubborn self. Whatever it turns out to be she just prays that she'll be understanding. We are entitled to react anyway we choose to rather right or wrong. We also as adults have the responsibility to tell someone if they offended them also.

Anyway, I'll worry about that later. I'm running late enough. I don't want to miss everything sitting here worrying about someone that clearly not worrying about me. I will take care of that when the opportunity presents itself. Right now, my future husband awaits.

*　　*　　*

"Whoa, whoa, whoa. Hello, hello?"

"Hello? Lawrence?"

"Yeah, who this?"

"Who this? That's how you answer the phone boy?"

"Boy! Yeah who is this?"

"It's me Lawrence so calm your attitude. I was just about to hang up"

"Who is this Chaz?"

"The one and only, she replied. What you've forgotten my voice now?"

"What's up baby girl? No, it's not that. It's that I had a crazy day so far. I'm just getting back from taking your girl to the airport."

"Oh really."

"So, what's been going on wit'cha?" Lawrence looked around the room. He realized he left his clothes all over the bed trying to find the right suit for his date tonight. That wasn't like him he always kept his place spotless. So much has kept him busy this morning, with Veronica leaving and all he almost forgot he had a date tonight. Man, he hoped Chasity kept this conversation short or he'll be running late himself.

"Nothing much," Chasity answered a little weary.

"From the sound of your voice you don't sound like you're having a good time. Is everything going ok?"

"Yeah, so far so good."

"You're sure? There was a brief pause on the other end of the phone. All Lawrence could hear was heavy breathing. He didn't know what to take from it. Chasity has been acting kind of strange lately, her unusual silence puzzled him. "Hello? Are you still there?"

"Lawrence, I think we need to talk."

"What about?" So many things started running through his head. What could it possibly be? She couldn't be in love with him she made that known a long time ago. So, that was out of the question. He knew she wasn't pregnant the last time they've had sex was a month ago, he had worn a condemn.

He had been trying to get her attention for years now but she had always pushed him away. So, he chose to move on. Yeah, they still messed around every now and then but that's about it. That's how she has always wanted things and that's how he has kept things for the past five years.

Her leaving town like this suddenly has been confusing to both him and Veronica. Hopefully she'll confine in him and he'll at least know what's been going on with her for the past week and why she just jumped up and skipped town without telling Veronica why she left.

"I want to talk about us."

"Us?" Why is she trying to play with my head he shouted! She knows there is no us. He stood up and started pacing the room. "What about us?"

"I don't know how to come right out and say it." Chasity was now a bit flustered. She noticed that he sounded upset when she brought up the word us. "To be honest Lawrence I'm having problems putting it into words."

"Well if you're that bothered by it then just come right out and say it."

Chasity was hesitant herself this time. She wasn't sure how he would handle her news. Lawrence had been known to over react to certain type of news in the past. What if he gets upset? What if he laughs? Better yet what if he rejects what she says? No, now is defiantly not the time. "I can't, at least not like this."

"Chasity you're losing me. I mean is it something I said or done?"

"No, it's nothing you said."

"Well, what did I do?" Man, this is a lot of bull I don't have time to be playing games. If you have something to say you should just come out and say it."

You made me fall in love with you... Chasity thought out loud. "I can't bring myself to talk about it now Lawrence. I promise you we will talk about it later. Okay?"

"Are you sure? I can tell whatever it is it's bothering you, but if that's what you want you know I'm here when you need me."

"Yeah, I'm sure. Now just isn't the time. See that's what I love about you. No matter what you always make yourself available to be my shoulder."

"Yeah, yeah."

"I'm serious. Thanks again for the offer babes."

"Suit yourself. Have you talked to Veronica?" Lawrence asked changing the subject.

"No, I haven't." Why did he have to bring her name up she asked. Things were going just fine without her name being the center of their conversation.

Lawrence could sense the anger in Chasity's voice when he brought up Veronica's name. He hadn't noticed that in her voice before and wanted to know why she hadn't talked to her best friend in a week.

"That's unusual, she's been asking about you. She stated that she hasn't heard from you in a week. Is something going on between the two of you?"

"Not really. I've just been very busy that's all. Why did she say something to you?"

"No, I was just asking. I just haven't seen you two go this long without talking and I thought something had to be wrong."

"Everything with us is fine. Nothing we can't handle. We've been girls for a while you know we go back and forth like this all the time."

"Hold on for a minute baby, one of my homies on the other line."

She could tell he didn't believe her. Even if she told him the truth about everything he still wouldn't understand so why even bother.

"Ok I'm back. So, how's the conference going?"

"Don't you mean a bunch of lectures?"

"Is it like that?"

"Yes. All I've been doing all week is listening to different doctors and speakers since eight am. All of this sitting is about to drive me crazy!"

"What about the doctors you were bragging about to me yesterday? I can tell they had your nose wide opened?"

"Those tight wades? Most of them walk around with rods stuck up their butts or books stuck in their faces. The other half are walking around acting like the untouchables. All everyone act like they have time to do is stay in their room eat, drink and study. I don't even have time for that drama. We are here in Miami and nobody wants to go to the clubs for drinks or nothing. I just don't understand it. There has to be decent man out there somewhere."

"So, you say they're feeling themselves huh?"

"Pretty much. So, what do you have planned for tonight?"

"Well I have a date with Naomi. For starter's I'm taking her out to a nice romantic dinner to a five-star restaurant and then we'll see where it goes from there."

"I know you didn't just say you were going out with big breasted Naomi?"

"What's up with you and Veronica when it comes to Naomi?" Lawrence questioned.

"We know a whore when we see one."

"Now you know that was way out of line. I'm actually not surprised that you would say something like that but now you got Veronica talking like that as well."

"Well we all can't keep that good girl persona forever Lawrence."

"You mean to tell me there's more things about you that I don't know huh?"

"There could be."

"Like what?"

"Never mind. Forget I said it."

"No, I want to know what you meant?"

"Just forget, she stated now embarrassed. Change the subject!"

"Ole Miss Chasity Simms is finally letting down her guard."

"What does that supposed to mean?"

"I'm just saying that you're finally letting go of that wanna be good girl persona you had."

"Well I can't stay that way forever."

"I see that now"

"Stop smiling"

"What?"

"I can feel you smiling through the phone."

"Ole Miss Cha-si-ty."

"Shut up will ya." He could be so silly she needed that laugh from him today. He always knew what to do to lighten the mood. It was just like clockwork. That's what's she loved about him.

"I'll leave it alone for now. Hold on I have another beep."

"Alright" I love Lawrence so much but how can I tell him that I'm madly in love with him. I have been in love with him for going on four years now. What could I say to him about the situation that wouldn't make him run away or hate me? I'm sure his first question would be why now after all this time? Why not now? Why do I have to put a time limit on my feelings?

All I know is that I love him more than anything and I want him to be with me. I know that may sound selfish but I don't want Veronica to have him. She had her chance a long time ago but she blew it. Now it's my chance to take back what rightfully belongs to me.

Then again, she is my best friend. How can I tell Veronica that I'm hatin on her because he's in love with her? I often wonder are these feelings I'm having worth losing my two best friends over. Lord, I need some answers.

"Hello Chaz? You still there?"

"Yes, I'm here."

"Well, baby I have to go it's an important call I have to take. Call me back tomorrow."

"Okay babes. Love you."

"Love you too. Call Veronica ok."

"Okay." There he goes again. Why does he always has to be so concerned about her. I'm just as important.

"I'm serious she needs to hear from you."

"I will you have my word."

"Alright. I'm out later."

"Later." There must be a way to tell him how I feel without ruining our friendship. I going to have to tell him sooner or later no matter what. Either I tell him now or risk him and Veronica falling in love and getting married later.

"Doctor Simms, you're wanted in conference room two."

"Okay I'll be right there."

*   *   *

The countryside was beautiful this time of year. You vividly see the view of the mountainside from the entrance. That was her first time driving up to the country club by herself. She had tagged along with her dad when she was younger. Driving by herself she had to admit felt a little weird. It was apparent that she was late, she was the only person pulling up in the parking lot. Thanks to Lawrence now Veronica had to hear her mother argue about her not showing up on time. It doesn't matter what she says, I'm here now and I plan on making the best of it.

Veronica was so nervous she could feel her hands starting to sweat. Oh, no I know I've forgotten something, I left my medicine home. I pray I do well without it. Hopefully I won't have to shake too many people hands that would make them swear more. Why did I have to be born with Hyperhidrosis? I guess that's why my mom treats me funny. She looks at it as if it's a disease instead of simply sweaty hands.

Anyway, enough about her, I am totally at owe. I can't believe I am here finally attending my first golf tournament. I almost thought the lady at the front gate wasn't going to allow me to come in. She stated that after a certain time she's not supposed to permit anyone to get passed the gates. I had to constantly inform her of who my father was before she even considered letting me pass. My dad's name has a lot of clout in this line of business thank God. She said the first round was just about over and I pretty much missed everything. There wasn't a need for me to waste my time going inside. I informed her that I was meeting my family inside so I might as well. I'm ok if Warren is still here I don't think I've missed a thing.

Look at all of this! I feel like a child a carnival for the first time. The greens look amazing, up close it looks like well-groomed carpet. All the different colors of flowers were also beautiful to look at. There are so many people walking around everywhere. Whenever I've watched the tournament on television it didn't seem as if so many people were here all at once.

There was a nice breeze coming through the trees that made you feel like you were on a tropical island. I'm not sure if that was the air coming from the atmosphere or the fact that it was close to one hundred degrees outside.

Veronica was looking around. She wondered where Warren could be? I can't wait to see his handsome face she thought. During times like these is when she misses her best friend Chasity. She was the one that would make this occasion fun. She would do something crazy and outrageous to get attention or she'll flirt with every man there getting most of their phone numbers. While I'll be somewhere hiding trying my best not to show that I was embarrassed. There was a young attractive lady coming towards her direction she figured she would ask her what hole Warren was on to keep from pulling out her phone.

"Excuse me ma'am could you tell me what hole Warren Beasley is currently on?"

"Unless you were dumb enough to had just gotten here you would know that he was on the seventeenth whole."

"Hold up! I was just asking a question you didn't have to get smart about it."

"And I answered you question." She added with a fake smile.

"Let me let you go before I end up saying something nasty to you."

"So, we're done?"

"Yes, I guess so."

"You have a nice day ok hun."

"Whatever." Veronica turned and watched this very blonde beautiful lady with a very nasty attitude walk away. What was that all about she questioned? All she did was ask her one question and she flips her wig. You would think she asked for his phone number or something. Then again that heffa did look real familiar.

I had to calm down I thought I was about to lose it for a minute. I wanted to snatch her fake extension off that head. She looks like she was the type that would've given it back. Oh well she had the right one today. I don't care where you go I see there are crazy people everywhere.

That's all I would need for something to pop off and my mom would find out about it. She would be on me so fast it wouldn't even be funny. Not to mention Val mouth would also be running a mile a minute.

Ok I need to just shake that off I can't allow her to ruin the remainder on my evening. Veronica knew after that delay she needed to hurry up to the eightieth hole before she missed Warren. Where could her family be, she wondered? She hasn't received not one call from them since she landed. Maybe they think she changed her mind. She knows her mom is somewhere either bragging about her super model sister or getting on her dad's nerves. She just prays that her dad could stomach it all and not allow her bother him too much at least until we arrive.

As Veronica, approached amen corner she saw a very attractive male walking towards the greens. Far away she could vaguely see his face because he had his head down but she was sure it was Warren. The closer and closer she gotten to him she was certain it was Warren Beasley. Veronica instantly felt her heart fall directly to her shoes it was beating so fast. She couldn't believe she was standing that close to him. She didn't know rather to run, jump or scream, but just standing there didn't seem like an option.

He is so gorgeous, she couldn't help but smile when she seen him. Look at that caramel skin glistening in the sunlight and those soft red juicy lips. She felt her inside flush as he passed by. How did she end up on the front line when she tried to hide on the second line she had no idea? However, it came to be now she was standing directly in front of him.

She was embarrassed for showing up there late. There's no way he could possibly remember her out of all those people but she knew she hadn't seen not one piece of his round that day. So, how could she stand here on the front and pretend like she's been there the entire time. She tried her best not to draw attention to herself like her outfit didn't help. Every time she tried to go back to the second row someone would purposely push her back to the first row. She wasn't sure but it was almost as if someone was doing it on purpose.

When Warren walked by to retrieve his ball he looked up and gave Veronica a glance and smiled. She had to look around to make sure was looking at her. Hot flashes started coming from everywhere when she realized that he was smiling at her. She felt her knees getting weak but she was still trying to remain cute all at the same time. Ok Veronica you must keep your cool she thought.

Ok she knew now that she had gotten his attention. So, the next time he looked up she decided to return the smile. She slyly smiled back this time just a little seductively. She laughed when he almost dropped his putter pretending he was trying to measure his put.

To mess with his head a little bit she decided to stick out her leg to get his attention. Not to distract him but to give him something to look at while he putted. He was trying to act as if he hadn't noticed but she knew he had. After all he's a man they always look.

Even though she had worn a hat it was still scorching hot out. She asked this elderly lady could she share some of her umbrella? She smiled and gestured for Veronica to come over. She was happy that there were still some nice people still in the world. Other than that crazy woman that she ran into earlier.

His ball was about fifteen feet away from the hole, that was a makeable putt for him. He needed one more birdie to finish in second place with five under par for the day, one shot behind the leader.

A man walked around and asked us all to quiet down before he made his putt.

It was a great hush over the crowd as he raised his putter. You could almost feel how intense the air was it was so still. We all waited with anticipation for him to make his shot. Right when he raised his putter for the second time a crazed fan shouted "In the hole Warren. You're the man."

Veronica was so upset she started to head over there and slap him in the face. Security made over there and quickly asked the man to either quiet down or he would be asked to leave. The looked offended at first but he quickly calmed down. "Some people don't seem to have any proper home training do they baby?" "No, ma'am, they sure don't." Veronica responded with a smile.

She noticed that Warren never lost his concentration. He remained the exact same way throughout the whole ordeal. That made him look even more attractive and strong. He raised his putter for the final time and the ball went in. The crowd irrupted. You would've thought he won the tournament the way the crowd was carrying on. It was easy to see that he was the crowd favorite that weekend and hers as well.

Warren was finished for the day. The crowd that was around him started to disburse. Everybody was following him towards the playhouse she assumed trying to get pictures and autographs. She was supposed to meet her parents and sister there also, so she might as well head that way herself.

There were a lot of people standing around waiting to get his autograph and picture. She was also one of them. She didn't care about receiving his picture she just wanted him. Since she couldn't get him yet she'll just settle for a picture.

Women standing in the front starting giving her weird looks. She understood she weren't dressed like everyone else but there were no reasons for those looks. There was no way she was going around dressed like most of the women there. Their closed were boring and very cliché. Besides she was a designer, she had an image to uphold she protested.

Oh well they'll get over their selves. About twenty minutes had passed when she was about to say forget it. It was very hot outside and it felt as if the temperature was climbing by the minute. The weather man said it would be close to ninety-five today and she wanted to be inside out of it. No man is worth standing out in all this heat.

The crowd started to get rowdy just as she headed for inside that meant Warren must be on his way back out. Veronica tried moving closer in front of the crowd to get a better look but got knocked all the way to the very back of the line. He was standing directly in front of the club house, the only way to get inside were to walk directly pass him.

There was no way in the world she was doing that she argued. He can't take pictures forever she thought. About ten minutes had passed and it was getting warmer and warmer. He was still taking pictures. Does he ever get hot! I mean really. Veronica wasn't used to this type of weather, she was about to pass out. She finally said forget it and head inside for something cold to drink.

On her way inside she passed him as perceived to take pictures with his many admires. She knew she had to do something to get his attention again. This time she decided she should speak. "Hi," she smiled. He just smiled and continued taking pictures. Ok I feel stupid she thought. I went through all of that and all I got was a smile and a nod. Really? She didn't know how to feel after that. She knew for sure that going inside was her best bet to get past the embarrassment she just endured.

Her hands were sweating uncontrollably from all the excitement that she could barely open the door. She pulled out a handkerchief wiped her hands and used it to open the door to get inside. Once inside she took a long awaited deep breathe. She tried her best to suck in all the cool air she could. The lounge area was as rowdy as the outside. There were media and reporters everywhere. If her sister where there she would be in heaven.

She walked around until she found a bar. She was so thirsty she ordered a large ice water with lemon. Something stronger would be nice after what had just happened but it was way too early and hot for that. Water for now would have to do. Before Veronica could get her thought out she looked and seen Warren walking through the door.

Where in the world did he come from that quick? She almost slipped of the stool trying to sit down in her romper. She tried to turn around and hide her face pretending as if she hadn't seen him hoping he wouldn't notice her.

Where in the heck is her family? Any other time if she didn't want them there they would be somewhere harassing her. "Ma'am can I get you anything?"

"Huh? Who me?"

"Yes, I asked if I could get you anything?" asked the bartender

"Um yeah, sure. I'll take a large ice water with lemon please. Thanks"

"I would like the same," she heard a strong voice say coming from beside her.

"Yes sir Mr. Beasley coming right up."

Veronica was afraid to turn around. She knew for a fat her ass would for sure come crashing from off that stool. She was now sweating places she didn't need to sweat. She immediately felt herself start to feel lightheaded. He was now standing right next to her and she didn't have a word to say. She could feel the warmth of his breath on her neck he was now standing so close. The sweet smell of his cologne was starting to tickle her nose as she tried not to look in his direction. She vowed to never to forget that scent ever. She could almost feel hear her heartbeat as he reached over to get a napkin as he lightly brushed her breast.

He was even finer than before. It was harder to look at him up close than it was when she could only glance at him outside. She tried her best not to fall off the stool as she slowly turned to face him.

"Hi again." He said with that same wonderful smile.

"Hi," was all Veronica could manage to get out of her mouth.

"Nice day we're having huh?"

"Sure, if you're a fan of really hot weather."

"My name is Warren, he said extending his hand. And you are?"

Veronica stared at his hand for seemed like hours. Her hands already felt like they were dripping with sweat. She couldn't possibly shake his hand now. He still had his hand extended but he started to get a little offended when she didn't reciprocate. To keep from offending him she shook his hand anyway.

"Veronica Martin. Nice to meet you. I apologize my hands are so sweaty I…"

"It's ok you're fine. Nothing a napkin can't take care of. So, do you come here often Ms. Martin?"

"Now that is funny. That is such an original. Did you think of that all by yourself?"

"I had to think of something to say to you. That's all I've come up with since the first time I've laid eyes on you."

So, he did notice me, ok. "Really, I'm impressed. I see you put a lot of thought into it."

"Cute that's funny," he smiled.

She could barely hear anything he were saying. All she could see were those juicy lips of his moving up and down. If only she could be the cold water he was drinking. She thinks he noticed her staring because he suddenly turned red and slyly stared smiling.

"I see you enjoyed the end of the tournament."

"Well yes and no." She tried to catch herself from slipping off the stool. The heat from him being so close and the heat from outside was making it hard to stay seated.

"Are you ok? He asked with a raise brow. I don't understand was it yes or no."

"Yes, I'm good. I'm embarrassed to say I was late getting here."

"I know."

"How could you possibly know I was running late when you were playing golf the entire time?"

"I know but I still noticed you. You're not hard to miss dressed like that. Not to mention I think you're very beautiful."

Ok is he boldly flirting with me? For the past couple of weeks, I rehearsed what I would say if something like this would happen. Now that it has and I have nothing to say back. I am a total loss of words. Veronica you need to get it together girl I mean fast. Say something, anything! If I keep sitting here grinning he's going to think I'm crazy.

"I'm flattered."

"Why?"

"Why what?"

"Why are you flattered? I'm sure you here stuff like that all the time.

"Yeah but not always from the right people but I never get tired of hearing it"

"Well I never get tired of saying it."

"Mm hm my throat is extremely dry. What about yours? I could use a drink of water."

"Is this your first time here?"

"Yes, it is. I'm here with my family on vacation. My dad is a huge golf fan and a huge fan of yours we decided to come here instead of the Virgin Islands."

"Wow! Now I'm flattered."

"You may have heard of my father Richard Martin, of Martin's A Set Above Golf Apparel. He also currently has his own line of golf clubs coming out soon as well."

"I've had the pleasure of meeting you father a couple of months ago on Richmond VA he's a very nice man."

"Well, thank you. He's the best dad you could ever ask for."

"So, how long are you here for?"

"We're here for a week. Then it's back to work for me as usual."

"What do you do for a living?"

"I own my won clothing business. Well me and my best friend Lawrence. We own two boutiques and the warehouse that manufactures the clothes."

"Really, that sounds interesting," he added. I've noticed that he kept looking over his shoulders as if he was looking for someone. Am I starting to bore him? I didn't think that was talking that much.

"If you have somewhere to be don't let me keep you?"

"No, you're fine."

"Are you sure?"

"Yes, 'm sure. So, what the name of your company?"

"It's called L&V Apparel."

"Has a nice ring to it. What made you come up with that name?"

"Lawrence and I just combined our first initials. We wanted something simple but jazzy."

"Cute, added with a raise of eyebrow. I see this Lawrence character is someone you spend a lot of time with?"

"Well, yeah. We are business partners."

"I see."

Why would he ask about Lawrence? He doesn't even know me nor Lawrence for one to be asking in my business like that. And to be questioning me about how much time we spend together, that's different.

Before I could respond to his question a beautiful young lady walked up from behind us. I almost felt myself getting jealous for a minute. I wanted so bad to ask who she was, but decided against it.

"Excuse me Mr. Beasley I'm sorry to interrupt but you're now wanted in the conference room.

"Okay thank, I'll be right there. Well I guess I must get going. I don't want to keep them waiting. Will I see you later at your dad's fund raiser?"

"Sure, if he doesn't have us too busy running all over the place. Other than that, I will be right there."

"Will I see you before then?"

"Um no, I have plans."

"I understand. Well I guess I will just have to see you tonight then."

"No, I didn't mean to say it like that. It's just that I'm meeting my family for dinner right after this that's all. You know how that is."

"Yes, I really do understand."

"Well, I'll see you tonight then it was a pleasure meeting Ms. Martin, he extended his hand. Really, he wants me to shake his hand again? Not this time. I'm already perspiring like crazy. This time he's going to have get a huge.

"It's nice to meet you as well." Veronica leaned in a gave Warren the biggest hug she has given anyone in a while. She's not sure how it made him feel but it made her feel good to have her arms wrapped around his strong shoulders finally. He didn't hesitate nor pulled back. That made the situation seem even more pleasurable and both awkward.

"Well, I must let you go now. Don't want to keep them waiting any longer than we have," Veronica added slowly stepping back.

"Ok, I'm really looking forward to seeing you later. Before she knew it, he leaned over and gave her one of the sweetest, yet softest pecks on the forehead. He lips felt so soft they made the temperature go up she knew another ten degrees. It was already hot enough to make her pass out it didn't need to get any hotter. It took everything in her not to scream as she watches him disappear around the corner.

Just like that it was over. He was gone. This entire day so far is turning out to be so weird. I need somebody to pinch me because I must be dreaming she reasoned. There's no way none of this could be real. Never in my wildest dreams would've I've thought something like this would happen. Yes, my dreams about him has been wild but this takes the cake.

If things go as well as she hopes they will be sharing more than a kiss on the forehead. Veronica could barely get her thoughts together when she seen her mom and dad coming around the corner. She suddenly went from feeling happy and excited too sick to her stomach. Well, there goes the end of her perfect day Veronica said to herself, Miss know it all has now arrived.

CHAPTER 5

Meet the Martins

I was doing just fine hanging out with Warren before I've seen my parents coming around the corner. All the places located around the country club how in the world did they find me here?

Oh, my God look at her waving her hand like she has lost her mind. I wish she would stop that, people are starting to stare. I'm most certainly am not going to wave back. I don't want people to know that she's related to me. I wish dad would say something to make her stop. As perfect as she claims she is I can't believe she's carrying on like that.

I should have known she would be dressed just like everyone else her, just look at her. I sure she would have something negative to say about my outfit as soon as she lays eyes on me. She has no sense of style what so ever, she thinks she does. I'm a grown woman she can't tell me what to wear anyway. Lord, here they come.

"Hi daddy," she said giving him a kiss. I'm glad you made it here safely." Her dad was looking very handsome today for a fifty-nine years old man. Look at him in his dark blue and tan shirt she admired. He knows I'm feeling those matching khakis, I taught him well. Now her mother on the other hand she's dressed like everyone else. Everything must match from head to toe. First, you must wear the white Capris or khakis, the hat must match the shirt. The shoes must match the purse, your hair must be pulled back in a ponytail.

The most important thing on her list is to never forget your designer shades. See what I mean just like everyone else.

"How's my baby girl's doing?" Richard asked. You're having fun yet?"

"More than you could ever imagine," Veronica responded excited.

"Your father didn't come here by himself young lady."

Just the sound of her mother's alone voice made her stomach ache. Not to mention what the sight of her does. "Oh, hi mom," Veronica responded with revolt.

"Oh, hi mom? That's how you greet me now? Where's my hug?"

I really wasn't in a hurry to hug her. I think she could tell by the expression on her face. "Veronica Denise Martin you better give your mother a hug! What has gotten into you lately? I think we need to talk later."

Like she really needs to ask me what's my problem. She knows I don't like her. I love her because she's my mom, but she knows we don't get along. "I think that talk is well over due." I wonder what that talk could be about, but then again in away knowing her don't want to know.

"Okay enough about that, we didn't all come here to argue. We game here to enjoy our vacation and have an enjoyable time is that clear ladies?" Her dad asked.

"Yes, daddy anything for you," Veronica replied kissing her dad on the cheek.

"Debra?"

"Humph," Debra retorted.

"What was that dear?"

"Nothing Richard, nothing at all."

Someone is missing Veronica questioned. Now where is Miss Universe? She thought for sure she would be with her parents. Unless she thought she were too good to be seen with them.

"Dad where's Valerie? I thought her plane landed hours ago?"

"It did. As a matter a fact here she comes now."

When I turned around I saw this tall, slender, beautiful, woman with long brown curly hair floating around the corner of the vestibule. That was her sister Valerie Martin alright walking up like she was the Queen of England. We both had my dad's caramel skin but she was blessed enough to receive his tall slender body and sandy colored hair.

I for one inherited my mother's shape full breasts, hips and lips. People said my mother used to be a brick house back when she was younger. She still has a bad shape now but they said when she was younger she could give any woman a run for their money. I guess that's the only good thing I've inherited from her. Her personality sure wasn't one of them.

My sister on the other hand always looked like she came straight off the runway even when we were kids. Like I stated before because she inherited my dad's looks. My dad was a tall muscular man with a slender physique. I often seen women stare at him in awe that's how good looking he is. Even in his old age he is still considered very handsome. He has a wonderful smile and polite attitude that can draw people to him. You can tell that my mom is still very much in love with him because she still drools all over him. I can tell he feels the exact same way about her. They both can barely keep their hands off each other. He's constantly complimenting her, she's always complimenting him. I tell you just sicken.

The reason she favor's my sister so much could have a lot to with the fact that she looks just like my dad. Despite how beautifully my mother was shaped I somehow thinks she was secretly envious of my sister's body. I used to watch her stare at Valerie in the mirror while she was changing clothes when we were teenagers. She would stand there gazing at her like she was the most beautiful person in the world.

She watched me like that Veronica thought back. I don't think I was shaped like she like nor was I small enough. When we were younger she made sure my sister dressed in all the latest fashion and made sure she was dressed better than all the girls in the neighborhood. She made sure I was dressed nice as well but she thought that I was too tomboyish for her. She said I wore jeans and t-shirts too much for her. She Valerie carried her flair for glamour and fashion, that was something inherited not given. Back then she stated that somehow that trait must have missed me all together. Ha! What does she have to say now. I dressed better than them both. That's what made me decide to become a designer to prove her wrong.

I was what they called a late bloomer when it comes to doing anything especially when it came to looks. It took forever for me to come into my looks. Even at sixteen I still wasn't as fully developed as Valerie. I didn't even get my real first boyfriend until I was in the twelfth grade. Even he wasn't excited about the fact that I was still a virgin and was in no way in a hurry to let go of it. Come to think of it I have no Idea when Valerie lost her virginity. I know or fact she's no longer a virgin and I know most certainly she lost it way before she graduated high school!

When I finally came out of my shell I came out with a bang. My mother was just jealous that her shape turned out looking better on me. Instead on complimenting me on how good I was looking she started coming at me with the insults. She had the nerve to say if I didn't take care of my body when I get older that I could turn out looking like a saggy old woman. Now what was that to say to me at ten years old. I had no idea what no of that meant. At that times, I could've cared less about how my body were supposed to look. All I wanted to do then was play outside in the dirt. After that I just dismissed her as being mentally unstable for years.

I didn't know what to expect to come out of her mouth from then on out. After that we were never close, Valerie weren't close growing up either. Thanks to my mom she made sure it stayed that way. For the past two years Valerie has been in Paris modeling, I have been in Charlotte, NC running my clothing business with Lawrence and my mom and dad had been in our home town Mequon, WI. Where my mom stated that our families are originally from.

When I finally moved out of our home I kept my distance just going around on holidays and special occasions. Other than that, we all don't see each other much. Today has been the first time we have gotten together in two years. So, you can understand enthusiasm over this weekend. My parents seem to make a big deal about me not coming home, but thinks ok for Val to drop in and out of town every couple of years. I never could quite understand this family.

"Hey baby sis, "Valerie stated grabbing Veronica forcefully.

"Whoa, whoa I'm happy to see you too but you don't have to be so forceful about it."

"I apologize. It's just that I'm so happy to finally see you."

"Well I'm happy to see you too." Veronica responded surprised.

"How's my baby girl doing, Debra came running to Valerie's side. I missed you so much. How was your flight? Are you tired? Do you need anything to eat? Oh, I just missed you so much."

"Um mom we were just talking."

"You weren't talking about nothing. Besides I wanted to hug my baby I haven't seen her in a while.," Her mom added smiling ear to ear.

Richard stood back and watched it all for a minute. He never understood how Debra always chose favoritism when it came to his daughters. The way he saw it he loved his daughters both the same one was no better that the other. By looking at his expression Veronica could tell what he was thinking. He wishes Debra wouldn't react the way she does when they all got together. Always making one feel more superior over the other.

"Ok Deb that's enough. You're not the only one she came here to see."

"I know Richard I missed her so much, "she added looking in Veronica's direction.

Veronica tried very hard to keep her mouth shut. "What are you looking at me for?" I can't stand that woman sometimes!

"Deb?"

"What Richard? I hadn't said a thing."

"I don't know what to do with you sometimes, shaking his head. Hi Valerie baby. How was your flight?"

"It was long. I missed you too daddy."

"Glad to finally be home?"

"Yes. More than you know. Paris is an exciting place to live but nothing's better than being home."

"You bring us back anything from your travel?" Sounds like Lawrence Veronica thought.

"Dad you know I did. It's back in the hotel room, I'll give them to you later. So, what's on the agenda for today?"

"So where is this room located?" Veronica asked

"I'm rooming with you of course baby sis."

"What!" Valerie purposely ignored her and kept talking.

"I Should be tired but I'm down for doing anything right about now." I knew it stated Veronica. I should've known that second room were for one of them darn it. I can't stand Valerie but I'd rather that room be for her than my parents.

"For starters, I thought that we should have an early dinner before the fundraiser. I'm starving."

"That's fine with me, Valerie added. After flying for fourteen hours I could use something good to eat. It'll give us time to catch up on lost time."

"Times I think should remain lost."

"What was that Ronica?"

"Nothing." I honestly don't I have anything to talk to them about. I defiantly am not in the mood for sharing. She noticed that her mom was giving her weird looks. I wonder what's that all about?

"Veronica? Do you plan on wearing that?" questioned her mom.

"Yes I am. What's wrong with it, she asked looking down at herself.

"I just don't think it's appropriate."

"I agree with mom. The color is fine, but it's not appropriate for a five-star restaurant."

"I don't care I'm not changing. This is a designer original. If it was good enough to wear in here it's good enough to wear anywhere else."

"Oh, that's cute, you're still doing that little thing. I thought was just a phase you were going through I see you went and made a career out of it. That's right you're working with Lawrence now right. What's he's up to now and days? Is he still fine?"

"It's not a little thing it's my business that's doing awesome thank God. Lawrence and I don't work together we're partners and yes he's just as fine as he was when you broke up with him four years ago."

"I see you're still very sensitive."

"I'm not as sensitive as you think."

"Glad to hear that," Val added sarcastically rolling her eyes.

"I'm sure you are."

"Well suit yourself, her mom added. You are entitled to look however you want to look, it's your like you said designer original. Come over Val let mommy see how beautiful you look."

Thanks to them like always Veronica no longer felt like part of the family so she walked off. They completely ignored her and dad while they started chatting like two old college girlfriends. My dad came over and wrapped his arms around my shoulders. I buried my head in his shoulders trying my best not to cry.

"It's okay Peaches. You know how your mom can be when it comes to your sister."

"I know daddy, but why is she so mean to me?"

"God only knows baby. I wish I knew why. You stop letting them get to you. You're doing wonderful for yourself. You have a thriving up and coming business and you're about to open your third store. You have plenty to be proud of. Owning your business is just as spectacular as Valerie being a super model."

"How did you know that's what I was upset about?"

"Your hazel eyes are turning brown."

"Is it that obvious?"

"You're my baby girl I know you like the back of my hand. I know when you're hurt and when something is bothering you. You hold your head up high. You are a bright and intelligent woman. You don't have anything about your life to be ashamed of. I've always been proud of you even if Debra don't tell you enough. Now you give your dad a hug."

"Daddy you always know what to say to make me feel better."

"You know I can't stand seeing my baby hurt."

"What's all this," Valerie questioned a bit disturbed.

"Yes, Richard what is all of this about?" Debra asked furiously.

"It's nothing to make a big deal out of. Veronica was bothered about something and decided to confine in me that's all. Just a father and daughter thing."

"Well I'm the one that's just go in to town all of the attention should be on me."

"No Val you weren't the only one that just got into town Veronica did as well. She deserves just as much of our attention as well as you."

"Oh well. Did anyone get to see any of the tournament today."

"I've seen the end of today's round. Warren is in second place with five under par."

"Girl did you get a chance to see that fine Warren Beasley? He is one of the finest most eligible bachelors out there. Any woman in this world would be lucky to snatch him up. If I have my way he will be mine before this week is over."

"You meant if mommy has her way."

Oh, no she didn't Veronica wanted to scream. I see it's about to be on now. There's no way I'm letting that heffa and evil Debra get their claws on him. I should slap that smile right off her face. Ooh she makes me sick.

"Why are you looking at me like that? Oh, yeah I forgot you have a little crush on him."

"Who told you that?"

"You know mom tells me everything. How else do you think I keep up with things at home?"

I turned to face my dad who had this confused look on his face. He knew he was the only one I told about Warren. I guess he feels as if he had to tell his wife everything knowing she can't keep nothing to herself. How could he? I trusted him, I see you I can't trust anyone in this family.

"Well that's a lie I don't have a crush on him. I just love the way he plays golf." Her dad won't even look in her direction. Serves him right, he better look in the other direction. He's knows I'm going to kill him later.

"You don't have to be so offensive about it. There's nothing wrong with having a little crush on someone as handsome as he is."

"Well I don't."

"Suit yourself Veronica. Like I said it's not a big deal."

"Anyway."

"Well anyone hungry, blurted out Richard, I'm starving."

"So am I. I think I had enough of today's drama."

"How does Beverly Inn sounds to everyone?"

"Sounds good to me Deb. My treat to celebrate us all coming together."

"I guess it's Beverly Inn then, since nobody asked me what I thought?"

"God, you are being such a baby. Does everything as to be about you? It's the same thing every time we get together. If this is how you're going to act the entire time I'm better of spending my time resting in my room."

"I agree with Valerie. I see what you're trying to do and I'm not having it."

"But mom I..."

"But mom I nothing. I don't want to hear it. I'm still your momma and I want you to be quiet. You've done nothing but complain and show attitude since you've been here. If you didn't want to spend time with us then you should've stayed in your room no one made you come. Now we're going to Beverly Inn for dinner with or without you that's your choice. But your attitude stays here do I make myself clear?"

Veronica remained silent to keep from cussing. Her face was so red you would've thought it was on fire. I don't know who she thinks she is. How dare her speak to me that way. If she thinks I'm going to answer her she has another thought coming. She looked over and her dad was standing there with a blank look on his face. His silence let her know that he agreed with what her mother had said.

"Veronica Martin I asked you a question. Did... I... make... myself...clear?"

"Yes ma'am."

"Good now let's go."

"You're riding with us Peaches?"

"No, dad I think I better drive, "Veronica replied rolling her eyes.

"Suit yourself. I'll see you there," he kissed her on her cheek.

The three of them walked off without another word. If she thinks I'm going to let her get away with that she's sadly mistaken. I'm not about to let her embarrass me like that and get away with it. I see this weekend just got interesting. I can't wait to see what happens next.

*   *   *

I really needed someone to talk to right now. I tried calling Chasity, but all I kept getting was her answering machine. I guess she must still be busy. I'll call Lawrence and see what's he doing.

"Hello"

"Hey baby"

"Okay what's wrong," Lawrence asked giggling.

"Nothing. What makes you think something's wrong?"

"Ronica, you sound like you've lost your best friend. So, stop beating around the bush and tell me what's going on."

"I don't Know Lawrence. Sometimes I just want to ask God why did he put me with these people? I mean I just don't understand them. Like my mother for instance she's been on my case ever since she's been here. She acts as if everything that I do is so wrong. I mean what did I do to her?"

"What you're complaining about this time?"

"It's not that I'm complaining. It's just that my mom had the nerve to get loud with me today in front of her precious one."

"What? You mean the woman that birthed you into this world had the audacity to get loud with you?"

"See that's why I don't like telling you nothing. You're always thinking everything is so funny. Everything with you is always a joke. I for one didn't think it was ok for her to talk to me that way. I'm a woman grown not a child."

"Yeah but she's still your mother. You know to your parents it's doesn't matter how old you are you're still a child to them."

Veronica was at the stop light listening to Lawrence talk about what she thought was a bunch of gibberish. Nothing that he was saying could possibly make her feel better about her mother nor was the trip was turning out good so far. She had to switch ears while he was talking because he really was starting to piss her off. He always felt he had to agree with everything her mother said. That's why her family loved him so much he was always agreeing with them. It seemed like it was taking the light forever to change. The longer the light took the more she had to sit there and really listen to Lawrence's nonsense. She could still hear him in her ear "…you need to thank God you have a family that loves you… "…you need to stop being selfish and give your mother a chance… something, something, something, something was all she cared to hear. She completely toned him out the rest of the conversation. As far as she was concerned the conversation was over when he first went against her. "Hello Ronica are you still there? It sounds like you blocked me out"

"I hear what you're saying but my family has a lot of issues. To top it off my dad didn't even say a word to defend me. It was like he agreed with her."

"Maybe it's just you baby girl, and not your family?" Lawrence suggested.

"How you figure that?"

"Think about it. You've done nothing but complain about them yourself before you left North Carolina. It's like you were waiting for something bad to happen. You say they haven't given you a chance, when I think it's you who really haven't given them a chance."

"That's a bunch of bull Lawrence and you know it! I didn't make my mom say those nasty things she said nor did I make Valerie act the way she was acting. So, for you to have the nerve to say something that stupid really amazes me. How dare you blame me for not trying to put up with this family?

"Look like me you're trying to constantly blame them for your many hang ups. You really need to grow up and stop looking for someone to put all your faults on."

"You're right no one asked you." Veronica stated with conviction. "Besides who gave you the right to tell me how to react to something? This is coming from a man that thinks with his privates."

"For one this is not about me, I get along very well with my family. You called me complaining about how they're treating you so don't give me your attitude," Lawrence replied angrily.

I didn't have the stomach to tell him that he was right. All I've done was complain about was not wanting to see them before I even left North Carolina. I guess it really is me? Maybe I just need to give this week a little more time. Hopefully things would turn out a little better than I thought.

"Ronica why are you so quiet?" Lawrence asked suddenly.

"Maybe you're right for once, but don't let it go to your head."

"What? You're agreeing with me? I can't believe it."

"Are you really that surprised?"

"Yes, I am, and I'm loving every minute of it."

"You're not going to let me forget this, are you?"

"Not in this life time."

"You can stop grinning. I can actually see your teeth through the phone."

"Good. I hope you can also smell my breath as well, that's how wide my grin is," Lawrence added smiling.

"Well I doesn't matter I didn't call to argue with anyway. That's not going to make me feel better. I just really needed to hear a friendly voice. I had to call you since I still can't get in touch with Chaz."

"Really? That's odd I've talked to her earlier. She said she was going to call you."

"Oh!? What was she talking about? I mean did she even ask about me?"

"To be honest no she didn't ask about you at all. Actually, to tell you the truth whenever I brought up your name she would get an attitude."

"I don't know what about. I haven't done a thing to her. We haven't even been in an argument."

"Well baby I don't know what to tell you. All I know is that she was acting strange. She claimed she had something to tell me, but when I asked her what it about she just ignored me."

"Mm, I wonder what that could be all about? She really has been acting strange towards me too here lately." She has been known for doing some strange things in the past. But leaving and not telling us and keeping secrets. This is really out of character."

"I know even for her, and she has done some weird things in the past" Lawrence replied.

"Like when she ran off for a month to Vegas with a married man without telling us, and sky diving off a cliff and then just sending us pictures with a caption saying "not sure if you wanted to be here!"

"How about that Halloween she posed as a scarecrow in her yard and was scaring all the kids out of their candy."

"She did all of that because her lazy ass didn't feel like going trick a treating," they both busted out laughing hysterically.

"Yeah that's my girl, Veronica responded vaguely. I wish I knew what was going on with her."

"Hopefully she'll call you later and you'll get a chance to finally ask her. Then you may be able to get around to finding out what it is she has to talk to me about."

"The way she's been so secretive what makes you think she would tell me?"

"Aren't you two best friends? Don't you two share everything?"

"Um I guess not. Apparently, that may not be true for you neither. Aren't you also her best friend and she didn't even confine in you this time so you know I don't stand a chance. Besides you knew her before I did."

"True, true."

"Oh well, are you ready for your big breasted date? Veronica asked Lawrence sarcastically.

"Here we go again with jokes. I'm never going to get a chance to go out on a date with the woman if you and Chaz don't stop calling me. I also have a life to live you know. I don't have time to keep playing both of your psychiatrist all night."

"Oh! So now you got jokes huh? Anyway, what do you got planned for tonight?"

"I'm not telling you."

"Why not? You've always told me your plans before details by details. So, what gives?"

"Yeah, that was before I found out that you were psycho, he laughed. You might send someone to stalk us later."

"That is not funny"

"Believe me yes, it is. You've done it before in college remember?"

"That was college Lawrence. I was young and madly in love with you. I most certainly not neither of the two now. You still didn't answer my question."

"Which part of no did you not understand? And you know you still love me"

"Whatever and you know you're not being fair, I want to know" Veronica whined.

"Why is that so important?"

"Because the way things are going here you may be the only one getting some action tonight."

"Roni why should you care? Lawrence asked raising his voice. Aren't you still a virgin?

"Well yeah, Veronica responded with a sigh, I was hoping that would change before this week was over."

"Don't say another word to me." Lawrence responded angrily.

"I'm a grown woman I Have a right to make that decision."

"Ronica, I'm not saying that you don't but what you have is very sacred and it shouldn't be just thrown away on some golfer. If you want me to be honest you're the only woman I know that can still say that. So, consider yourself blessed. With all the diseases and stuff going around makes me wish I've stayed a virgin at times."

"Now that you put it that was maybe I need to think this through a little more huh?"

"Yeah you should, besides I want my wife to be pure when I marry her."

"Who told you I was marrying you?" Veronica asked surprised.

"I did, and you are. I'm not asking you I'm telling you you're going to be my wife."

"Not with all of the women you've been with I'm not. You must think I'm crazy!"

"Now that was cold. You really didn't have to say it like that."

"Well you just said yourself that it was a lot of stuff floating around out there. How do I know you haven't snatched something up for yourself," asked Veronica?

"You just have to trust me?"

"I'm sorry but I trust no one. I especially can't put my life in someone's hands by only going by hearsay."

"I feel ya, I feel ya. Well baby it's been real, I mean it really has but I have a date I have to get ready for."

"Yeah, yeah in other words you're tired of talking to me, right?"

"No, it's not like that, it's just that I have a date that I really would love to go on and I can't do that talking to you."

"Well go ahead then, just remember don't go swimming on this date tonight."

"Why not? "Lawrence asked suspiciously.

"Those breasts of Naomi's are so huge if you two go swimming you don't have to worry about drowning. Her huge breasts will surely be your floating device." Veronica stated laughing loudly.

"Bye Ronica."

"What?"

"I've had enough of your jokes for today. Good-bye!"

She managed to get I love you out before he hung the phone up in her ear. He'll be alright after all it's only Naomi. She's not really that important anyway. When it pertains to work only. I pray he don't use this date to mess that up.

I pulled up to the Beverly Country Inn it was just as lovely all the other building in this town. It was located right on the edge of town right next to the river. The scenery was just as enticing as from the balcony from my room. There was a huge water fall right across the street from the restaurant. I stopped to take a selfie in front of it before my family pulled up. I may never see anything this beautiful again so I wouldn't dare miss a chance to get a picture of it. It was beautiful outside for pictures though it was still hot outside. The sun was still beaming but it wasn't to the point I couldn't stand being out there. This side of town was a hot spot for tourist. There were people everywhere. I could barely get back to the inn when I spotted my parents car pulling up from around the corner. I ran up just in time to throw the valet my keys to my car as my parents was walking up to the door.

Immediately people noticed my sister just as soon as she stepped out of the car. They were stopping her asking for hugs and asking her to take pictures. I felt myself getting jealous watching the whole ordeal. For the first time, I wished it was me. Not one person asked me for a picture, a hug or nothing. Heck I would've settled for a good ole autograph. I don't think anyone even knew who I was. I even waved at one older lady and she just frown her face and rolled her eyes in the other direction. I started to throw something at her but I know for a fact that would've been lady like. Mommy dearest I know would surely have a pure fit.

My mom and dad stood there with a proud look on their faces. I know they were proud of their daughter. I don't blame them when you have a daughter that's a beautiful supermodel I would be proud of her as well. I literally can't stand my sister but I didn't say she wasn't beautiful. My problem is that she knows it.

I tried to stand there with them trying to act like I was happy and excited for her like they were but why fake it. My patience was really starting to wear thin. It was already hot outside and all this nonsense really made my temperature go up one hundred degrees more. I started to head for the door. When my sister pulled me by the arm and started screaming in my ear.

"Isn't this exciting Veronica!" she shouts excitedly. I haven't had a reception like this in years since I've been coming back to the states. Can't you just feel the energy?"

"Yeah all over," I proclaimed. I didn't mean to sound so bitter but I really could care less about how happy she was that people were paying her so much attention. I own my own clothing company and not once person said a word to me. She throws on clothes and slaps makeup on her face prances down a runway and everyone acts as if she done the most honorable thing in the world like ended world hunger. I can't remember the last time I've seen my parents that excited not even over me. It doesn't even matter it's not like I have anything to prove to them anyway.

I walked into the lobby of the inn as quick as could. I wasn't only because I was about to pass out I was trying my best to get away from all of them. When I peeped around the corner of the bar to see who was there the first face I saw was Warren's. Immediately our eyes connected. Suddenly I felt my body go into a trance. My stomach instantly started turning into knots. I felt nervous all over again. All I could do was smile trying not to look silly at the same time. No matter how fast I walked I couldn't seem to lose sight of his eyes. My sister noticed us looking at one another and decided to maneuver her way in front of me.

Her focus was to get his attention off me and onto her. As she passed by her she spoke and gave him this very seductive look that made my stomach turn. I was so upset I didn't know what to do. How was I supposed to top that? I wanted so bad to just walk by and pretend as if I hadn't even notice him, but to my surprise he spoke first. "Hi Veronica Martin," Warren spoke with a beautiful grin.

"Hi yourself," Veronica stated as she returned a warm smile.

Her mom and sister gave each other this weird look as if they were saying how did he know her name? She didn't dare say a word, she just smiled and kept walking towards her table. Eventually she knew she would have to explain herself because her dad was now giving her the same exact look.

"So, Peaches were there anything I missed at the tournament today?"

"We'll talk later dad I promise."

"Okay I'm going to hold you to that."

"I'm sure you will," she added grinning to herself.

"You ask me she did more than watch him play golf today, her mom state bluntly. I hope you didn't do or say anything to embarrass yourself and our family."

"I agree, added Valerie. I don't need my name all on the internet. It's hard enough for a model to keep a good name for herself as it is. For you to go ruining it would be bad for my career."

"First, no one asked you for your input when it comes to anything. I didn't do anything with or saying anything to Warren except for hello. Not that it's any of your business."

"I'm not about to get into this with you again Valerie responded with anger. You're starting to act like a baby all over again."

"Okay girls that's enough? Debra detested. Veronica you're starting to draw attention to us so I want you stop it. I mean right now!"

"Mom why are you yelling at me I didn't start this. You know what I'm tired of this day already. Let's just eat so I can go back to my room and get some rest", Veronica responded irately.

"Oh, stop acting like such a brat will ya," Valerie intercepted frowning her face.

"Mom did you hear that?"

"Yes, I heard it and I agree with what she just said. I sure hope you don't plan on acting like this the remainder of the time you're here. If so I'll rather you stayed in your room or spent your time doing something else." Debra interjected as she walked away from the girls.

Veronica just threw her hands up in the air shaking her head as if she was saying I surrender. Nothing she said was right when it came to those two. When they together it was like trying to talk to two deaf people. At least with them you could get a word across with a hand slap or something. She wouldn't dare say anything else to make the situation worst people was already starting to give them looks.

They were finally seated and not a moment too soon. Things were once again starting to get out of hand. She noticed that whenever they got into heated arguments their dad always ignored them or just walked away. She felt it had to be hard for him all those years to live in the house with a bunch of women not knowing who side to take during an argument. They all wanted him to side with them knowing if he did that would only upset the other. Anyway, you took it for him I know it was a win lose situation.

The inside of the inn was as gorgeous as the other places Veronica has been to so far since she's been in town. The waitress sat them at a table near a huge picture window overlooking that same beautiful water fountain. The theme inside was like a country inn but with a modern touch. There were lovely colors of rich yellows, beiges, whites, and just a hint of orange that caught your eyes. The place setting was decorated with gold and orange arrangements with matching plates. They finished the table with glass goblets and platinum silver ware for the eating utensils. Even though she did want to be around her family any longer, she had to admit the place was worth dining.

They all sat down without a word. What was there really left to say they all thought. Veronica wanted to remain quiet. Right now, her mind was traveling back and forth from Warren's table and Lawrence. Richard just sat there pondering if he made the right decision planning the trip. The silence between them was starting to eat away at him, that somehow made him think that it all really was a mistake.

Richard hated to see the three of them fighting. Like always it was over nothing. He never understood why his wife and oldest daughter got together and ganged up on Veronica. She was always too valuable when it came to them two. They both would attack her at the same time like two pit bulls she never could stand a chance. As much as him and his wife has been through with the situation involving both girls especially Veronica you would think that she would be a little nicer to her. I see somethings are harder to get over than others. Well, he guesses his baby girl would have to grow a back bone this week and learn how to fight back. She should learn how to stop allowing them to get under her skin. Lord knows it has been a task for me over the years he thought. He knew he had to say something quick to break the ice. The air around them was getting thick.

"So, Valerie baby how are you home for?" he awkwardly. Debra glanced up at him side eyed as is she was saying now you finally decided to say something.

"About two and a half months," she acknowledged gleefully. Then it's back to London for Fashion Week."

"Really baby? That sounds exciting. I always wanted to attend fashion week. I'm so proud of you. You look so pretty in your white today," she just had to add.

"Thanks mom that's sweet of you."

"Veronica doesn't your sister look lovely today?'

Veronica quickly gave her mother one of the sharpest looks that could cut glass. I wish you would leave me crazy heffa she wanted to say so bad. But she chose to roll her eyes instead.

Valerie noticed her sister dismay from her mother's question and for the sake of argument she thought it was best the she intervenes. "Um, Veronica

you look beautiful as well. Who did you say the designer was again?"

"I didn't and thanks it's a designer original. I designed it especially for this vacation."

"So, little sis how's business going? You think I'll work for you one day?"

"Business is excellent. Sales has gone up forty percent since last year. I know if we had someone like you modeling our clothing line sales would be through the roof."

"I have to admit your designs are to die for. I received many compliments from the last gown I've worn of yours last year to the ball. Nothing but rave reviews."

"Really? That's nice to hear. You never told me that before."

"Oh. Well I was really busy afterwards you know how that goes right?"

"Valerie that was last year."

"Yeah, I know," she stated shrugging her shoulders.

"Well, anyway Valerie thanks for the complement and caring about how my business is doing. It's nice to know someone besides dad cares."

I don't get it Veronica thought why was she being so nice? Did someone threaten her when their backs where turned? She looked over and saw a big smile on her dad's face. From his expression, he must've been doing some serious praying in that corn he was sitting in. Mom on the other hand just stared at me with disgust. I'm sure she was still upset about that last comment I've made. I don't care she should trying being a loving and caring mother sometimes. Like always she just sat there with her nose up in the air with nothing to say.

The waiter finally brought our food out. I had poached salmon, Tuna with a salad and my parents both had a lobster. Once again, we sat there in silence and ate our food. I guess it's going to be a lot of this back and forth stuff going on if we're going to get a long on this trip. I tried to enjoy my food but I found myself staring into Warren's direction again. He and his family was only sitting five tables away from us. The place was rather large but he wasn't so far that I couldn't see him.

He even looked delicious while he was eating Veronica thought. I wish I could be his fork that was going back forth, in and out of his mouth. Every time he bit down on his food she would imagine that tightness of his jaw was like same tightness of his strong hands. She wishes she could feel those same strong hands gripping her just as tightly later. She was getting so excited she could feel her drooling on herself. She had to catch herself before anyone else at the table notices. She quickly got herself together but her eyes were still glued on him. Every time he looked up she would look away. They were seating directly within distance of each other. She knew he had to be staring at her just as much as she was staring at him. If only her family weren't here she thought. She would invite him to the bathroom she seductively fantasied chewing on her napkin.

"Veronica what in the world are you thinking about?' Valerie question looking at her sideways. Why are you chewing on your napkin like that? Do you need a toothpick or something?"

"Um no. Ah I'm good. Thanks." she smiles nervously.

Valerie squinted her eyes and stared at Veronica for a minute. "What Val?" Valerie then looked back in Warren's direction. Veronica almost fell out of her seat but to her dismay they had already left. That was also disappointing she thought.

"Are you ladies prepared for this evening? Richard asked. Please don't be late for this event. This fundraiser is very important to me so need all of you be on time and on your best behaviors." Deb?"

"Richard!"

"I'm just saying you have to lead by example I need you to promise me no fighting."

"Ok, Richard. Whatever you say. It's your night."

"I already have everything planned out for you ladies for the rest of the week. I even have a couple of spa day and shopping trips planned for you as well as many other things. How does that sound?"

"That sounds good to me. Anything that will get my picture taken and posted on someone's page."

Veronica completely ignored Valerie's response her mind was back on Warren. She wondered how her week was going to turn out. Could things really go in her favor for a change? She looked down at her phone and noticed that she had a missed call from Chasity. She was pondering if she should even bother calling her back or not. She's been acting so funny lately she wasn't sure if she should even waste both of their time. She would be more understanding if she had done something wrong to her but that was in no way the case. I mean they haven't even been in an argument or nothing. She thought their friendship was getting stronger but judging by her action this past week she's starting to wonder. I'll just wait and call her back later.

"On your phone, I see", Debra questioned. Who possibly could be more important than spending quality time with your family?"

"Mom if you must know it was a miss call from Chaz. I will just a call her back later."

"I see you two are still friends?"

"Yes, Valerie we are. Why wouldn't we be?"

"Oh, I just thought that was a college thing. I thought you two had out gown each other by now. Usually when most people graduate the go their separate ways"

"Well that was not the case for her, Lawrence and I. Lying. Our friendship is stronger than ever." I know I was lying through my teeth but there was no way I was about to tell Val the truth. That we haven't talked in almost two weeks now.

"Dad you mentioned that you had some things planned already for the week. Exactly what did you have for us in mind?"

"Well for starters I thought a friendly round of golf would be fun for us all at the beginning of the week. If Warren's not busy I could ask him to stick around and give us a few pointers."

"Sounds good to me Veronica smiled. I haven't played in years that would give me a chance to shake off some of this rust."

"I'm happy you're excited, I hope it's more because you're spending time with the family not only the fact that Warren is tagging along."

"Dad of course not. I most certainly would be more excited to be around family (lying)."

"Sounds great to me dad, chimed in Valerie, it gives me a chance to meet other very rich and exciting people in this town. Not to mention the single bachelors."

"That's right Valerie baby, I can see them all falling at your feet."

"I mean really? Why would they throw themselves at her feet? I not that serious."

"Veronica you shouldn't say things like that. Sounds me to like you're jealous."

"Of Valerie? Mom please, I have no reason to be jealous of Val. No one cares if she's a model"

"Super model Valerie added. I'm tired of you putting down my profession like it's no big deal. I love what I do and I can't help if I'm very successful at it. You on the other hand…"

"No finish your sentence. You on the other hand what?"

"Veronica let it go," their dad reasoned. He felt another argument stirring.

"No, dad not this time. I want to know what exactly she's trying to imply?"

"Ok that's enough you two! I've had about enough of your arguing. Every conversation doesn't have to result in an argument."

Wow really? Veronica wanted to scream. Out of all that's been said today now she wants to be a mom. Why did she wait to say something after her precious daughter insulted me?

"I agree with Debra you two act as if you hate each other. We didn't raise you to act this way towards each other. You are starting to make this a very short vacation already. I've sat here and listened to you bicker from the time you've laid eyes on one another. It's been two long years since you've had the chance to even hug one another. Anyone else would be glad to call either one of you their sister but not you two. Now I demand this nonsense between the two of you to cease. I flew to Texas to enjoy a wonderful vacation with my three favorite ladies in my life. Please don't make me regret wanting us to spend time together. Now you all are going to get along from this point on. Do you understand? Debra, you too!"

"Yes sir", they all said in unison.

"Now that's better. If you can't get along for yourselves at least do it for me. Ok?"

"Ok you're right dad. We have been acting like two teenagers. I'm willing to let it go if Veronica's willing?"

Veronica tried hard not to sound hesitant, but at the same time she didn't want to be fake about how she was feeling. But for the sake of making her dad happy she would rather go along with the nonsense for now. Anything to keep from constantly being blamed for the mischief that keep occurring.

"Ok dad I can do that for you. I'll be the bigger person and let it go."

"The bigger person, really Ronica? I don't understand you..."

"Ok that's enough. You're going to agree to disagree and that's final."

"I agree Richard. If they think for one minute that I'm...."

"Deb I love you but I don't need your input this time. I think those two are going to be just fine if you stay out of their conversations. They can't talk without you constantly barging in. Let them two be. They are sisters it's healthy for them to disagree from time to time. What's not healthy is when you think it's ok to take sides."

"Now Richard that is not true. I..."

"Before you get it out yes, it is. They don't need you constantly trying to draw a wedge between them. Like I said let them be. They will be just fine."

"Richard where is all of this coming from?"

"Like I said, let them be."

We both looked over at mom she had this blank stare on her face. It was almost as if she was in a state of shock. For once so was I. For one I couldn't tell if she was upset or pissed her face showed no emotion. It has been years since we've heard my dad react like this. Even longer since we've seen him silence her like that. That look on her face and this new-found silence is just what we all needed. Now if she stays like this the entire vacation I just might enjoy myself.

We sat I silence for about another twenty minutes. The sudden blow up from my dad seemed to calm the mood for everyone. I'm sure my mom had plenty to say in her mind but out respect knew she had better keep it to herself. The way dad just blew up I know she don't want to start and argument with him right about now.

After we finished our dinner Veronica felt she needed a break. She excused herself from the table to finally call Chaz back all at the same time trying to clear her head. All the disagreeing was giving her a headache. Some fresh air could really do her some good. She dialed Chaz numbers and hesitated to press send this time. She really needed to talk to her, she usually was the most stable one out of the two of them. She could use a friendly voice right now. Oh, well here goes nothing.

* * *

Chasity was in the conference room when she felt her phone vibrate. She looked at the caller ID and seen that it was Veronica calling back. So, she finally calls me back huh? I don't really care to talk now. Besides I'm in a meeting she would have to wait. Just when she was about to press end their director announced that they were done for the day. Great so now I have to answer her call. On her way, out the door she quickly pressed send before the phone hung up. "Hello?"

"Hey girl! What's up with ya? So, you finally answered your phone huh?" she hears on the other end of the phone. I don't know rather to be excited or cuss your behind out?"

"Hey bat'cha, responded Chasity trying to sound excited. She knew she wasn't excited to hear from Veronica but she wasn't about to let her know that.

"So, what's been going on with ya? I'm mad at you. Why didn't you tell me that you were going out of town hussy?"

"Hussy? Forget you she Chasity responded laughing. You will have to get over your anger hun. It was a last-minute thing (lying) I

82

had to leave very quickly. I meant to call you but I didn't have time with packing and all. I told Lawrence with his big mouth, I knew he would eventually tell you."

"You're right. I only had to ask him once where you were. He didn't even hesitate, Veronica stated laughing. He has no problem telling me everything.

"I'm sure he doesn't, Chasity murmured.

"Have you heard from him today?"

"Yeah earlier. He told me that he was getting ready for a so-called date tonight."

"Girl did he tell you who it was with?"

"Yes, girl that huge breast Naomi Thomas. What in world is wrong with him. Is our friend getting that desperate? I mean damn, she's pretty but he can do way better than that."

"I know I told him the same, but all he did was accuse me of being noisy and told me to stay out of his business."

"What! You're kidding me? I would've cussed him out for that."

"Mmm Hmm girl. Pissed me off. You know Naomi is one my head designers. If he messes this date up she could end up quitting, and that could ruin our business. Does he listen to me? No!"

"I know right. His ass will learn one day when he catches something. Stuff like this makes me sick to hear. I mean a man that fine deserves to be with a good woman that cares about him."

"Chaz if I didn't know any better you sound as if you think that should, be you?"

"Girl, that's insane. You know me and Lawrence have been nothing but friends since grade school. Him and me? Girl please!"

"I was just saying. But I do agree, he does deserve to be with a nice decent woman for a change. Wouldn't it be something if he turns out to be the first one that settles down?"

That would mean the world to me Chasity thought. "Yeah, that would be something."

"We'll I didn't call you to talk about him. I want to know what's been wrong with you lately?"

"Wrong with me? What makes you think something is wrong with me?"

"This is my first time talking to you in almost two weeks. You went out of town without telling me. I mean did I do or say something wrong."

"Veronica what actions you've noticed from me that has caused you to say such things?"

"Ok, for starters you haven't been returning nor answering my calls. Secondly, you didn't tell me you were leaving, what was I supposed to think?"

"Veronica honestly nothing is wrong with me. Like I've stated before it was just something that came up at the last minute that's all. As far as not returning your calls. Every time you've called me I was in one of those long boring conferences. You know how those can be?"

"Ok Chasity if you say so."

"Seriously, don't let it get to you ok? It's nothing just let it roll off. You can now ease your nerves. Anyway, changing the subject. Have you run into that fine Warren yet?"

"Chaz, you wouldn't believe it but yes! I have even went as far as having a conversation with him."

"Girl stop! You're kidding. So, what is he like? Is he really that gorgeous in person?"

"Gorgeous is an understatement. He's just plain fine."

"So, what did you two talk about and don't leave nothing out?"

"We'll to be honest he's a really sweet guy, at least he seems sweet." We basically made small talk so far. Before we could get deep into our conversation, this lovely light complexioned woman came and swooped him up."

"You didn't get jealous?"

"No, I think she was only someone that worked there. I don't think there was a reason to make a huge deal out of it."

"Oh, well you're a better woman than me. Anyway, what else happened?"

"Nothing much after that. Even though everything was short lived I don't think I would ever forget it."

"Mmm I'm sure you won't. All I want to know is did he make you moist?"

"Chaz, girl when I sat next to him I was so nervous I nearly fell off the stool."

"Stool?"

"We were at the bar silly."

"I was about to say. What kind of freaky stuff were you two doing? Ok continue."

"It was so surreal. I almost wanted to pinch myself to make sure it all was real. He even gave me one of the sweetest kisses on my forehead before he parted the first time."

"All that happened from a five second conversation. Well damn I wonder what might had happened if you've stayed together longer."

"Ha! Anyway, I still thought that it was sweet."

"After all of that I would too. But I'm not mad at ya. You better do it hunni!"

"I know. I'm praying by this weekend is over it turns into something much more."

"Well time will tell. All I know is that your behind better not punk down. Looks like somebody may not be coming back still a virgin."

"I don't know. He might be the one that finally gets it."

"Be careful, you know how those celebrities can be."

"I know Chaz, I'm not stupid. I'm an adult I can handle myself."

"Ok, I'm just saying."

"I know you're just concerned, but I'm telling you not to be. I got this."

"Well handle yourself hunni. Have fun doing it. Something like this only happens once in a life time."

"I plan to do just that. Did I tell you that he was right here in the same restaurant that we're in."?

"No! Shut up. I mean you two keep running into each other. That could mean something."

"Only time would tell."

"Hold up you said we. So, you mean to tell me that the whole family is there also?"

"Unfortunately, yes…"

"Judging by the sound of your voice I can tell that things aren't going so well."

"Chaz that is an understatement. Everything that could go wrong has since the time we all laid eyes on one another. We even made my dad upset. Now you know how hard that is to do."

"Wow, things have to be really bad."

"Yes. It's way too much to tell over the phone. We will have to play catch up when we both get back home."

"No problem. Well baby doll I have to be going. I have some-things to prepare for tomorrow, not to mention I'm starving."

"Ok, I understand. Thanks for finally talking to me and listen-ing to me blabber for the past thirty minutes."

"You know I don't mind talking to you. You're my girl. Well let me go. Try to enjoy your vacation and you better come back deflowered."

"Ha! Yeah right over Lawrence's dead body. Girl he had the nerve to tell me that I was going to be his future wife so he wanted me to remain pure."

"Really? Humph." There was dead silence over the phone for a couple of seconds. Chasity usually would've thought that joke was funny but not today. She tried everything to keep from letting Veronica know just how she felt about her stupid comment. She wishes she would've kept what Lawrence had to say to herself. "Well let me go."

"Ok hun love you."

"Love you too. Bye."

"Bye." I'm so pissed off I don't know what to do. Why would he tell her something like that knowing she would come back and tell me? I can't believe him. Now he's making what I want to tell him harder and harder to say. How am I supposed to follow him saying she's going to be his wife? Ha! Over our dead bodies. I'll be damned if I would ever allow that to happen. Best friends huh? Yeah, I bet Mr. Lawrence Weldon. We'll see just how close we all will be once I've disclosed my news.

CHAPTER 6

The First Date?

Man, I thought I won't ever going to get rid of those two. Not to mention If I received one more phone call I was going loose it. Sometimes Veronica and Chasity makes me feel as though I have two wives instead of two best friends. It's already hard enough to date as it is, I don't need two extra women tagging along on my arms making things even more difficult. Every time I meet a woman I have to hide her from them to keep from sabotaging the relationship.

Like my date tonight with Naomi. To me shorty is fine as hell, booming body, nice breasts, she's extremely beautiful, she always looks nice. Oh, yeah and she's smart what more can a man ask for? So, what if she's the head designer of our company, I personally see nothing wrong with it. Veronica makes a huge deal out of everything. I know in the past I've dated a lot of the women within the company, things hadn't turned out well, but who can blame me for those? I damn sure didn't make them give it up, it's not my fault they all were easy prey.

I quickly found out that if you're the boss and have money women would do almost anything for a raise. So, all it took was a dinner and a good talk game and I was in. Like this date tonight. It only took me one attempt and her less than five minutes to accept my dinner proposal. So why are they even coming at me? I can't help it if I'm the man.

Lawrence knew Naomi worked with him but she wasn't like just any other woman. Although she liked to wear tight and revealing clothing she still was considered classy he really wanted to impress her. He wanted to take her some place high class and expensive. You never know Naomi could be the one.

He spared no expense on this date. He even went all out when it came to his attire. He decided to wear his black fitted silk Armani suit, with a white crisp silk button down opened shirt. No tie tonight he wanted to be extra sexy. To top it off a pair of black Italian Stemar boots and a silver Rolex sports watch. Lawrence was very materialistic when it came to dressing nothing was ever too much nor over the top for him. To really impress her he asked his valet to bring around his favorite silver sports car that he only driven when he wanted to impress certain dates.

He pulled up at Naomi's gated apartment building and buzzed for her to let him in.

"Who is it?"

"It's Big Daddy."

"Whatever." Naomi giggled. Come on around. It's the third building on the right.

Lawrence pulled up to the side of the curb of the building. He wanted to be a gentleman so he decided to get out and wait for her on the side on his car. It was nice and quiet where she lived. It seemed as if you had to have money to live there as well. Judging by the way a woman like Naomi carried herself he was not surprised. Finally, after about three minutes later a tall beautiful chocolate brown woman came strutting from around the corner. She was wearing a soft pink short mini dress with matching strapped high heeled sandals that went up her legs. She wore very soft pink makeup and her hair was bone straight and lightly flapping in the wind. She was a dangerously curvy woman, with breasts and a booty that was making it very hard to maintain his manhood.

She walked over and gave him a soft kiss on the lips. I'm not sure what type of perfume she was wearing he thought. But she smelled so damn good I started to say forget dinner and take her back upstairs and make her dinner. Then again, he was like nah, that's how most of his dates turned out and he wanted this one to be different.

"So, big daddy, Naomi whispered, where do you have planned for us to go?"

"Shoot, anywhere you want to go you keep that up."

"No, seriously. Where are we going?"

"Ok, I've made reservations at a very nice restaurant if that's alright with you? If not we can always go someplace else"

"No, that actually sounds nice. Ooh look at you! You look so handsome."

"Thank you, baby, you look very um, beautiful yourself." Lawrence stated trying his best not to say nothing stupid. In his mind tasty, you look like you taste like frosting, was the first things that came to mind.

Naomi looked up at Lawrence and he had this huge grin on his face. "What?"

"Nothing. It's nothing. You're ready?"

"Sure, if you are."

Lawrence opened the door for Naomi watching every inch of her curves as she walked passed him to get in the car. All he could say to himself was damn she was fine! Now all he had to do was get through the night trying not to solicit sex, not to think about sex, and trying not to have sex all before bringing her back home. Now how's all of that was going to happen he had no idea.

It was a nice warm evening so he decided to let the top down on the convertible and just cruise all the way to the restaurant. He had made the reservation for thirty minutes earlier so they weren't in no real hurry. He had the radio on some light jazz to set the mood. He looked over and Naomi was laying back in the seat looking very sexy he may add. Yeah, he chose the worse night of all nights to be a gentleman. If she only knew what was going through his mind right about now.

They were on a dark road with no cars coming, her on the stirring wheel, slow jazz playing whoa Lawrence man keep it together.

"Um you ok over there baby?"

"Mmm hmm." was all he heard. Dammit woman you are not helping! He thought. To keep his composure, he just cranked the music and just cruised the rest of the way there. I wonder what Veronica is doing right about now. She hasn't called me for a couple of hours now. Either she's really enjoying herself, she's killed her mom, or her mom has killed her. I just hope she's nowhere near that Warren character. As far as I'm concerned, I think he's joke. She can do far better. What women see in rich athlete like that anyways? All I know is that she better come back home a virgin, I don't give a damn about nothing else. Or she'll have me to deal with.

Lawrence kept checking his phone almost seemed like every three minutes to see if he had received a text from Veronica. Nope still no call or text. Man, he wanted to throw the phone.

"I've noticed you keep checking your phone. Are you expecting a call?"

Lawrence looked over trying his best not to catch a major attitude. "Nah, I just thought I felt my phone vibrating."

They finally reached their destination. By that time his attitude has calmed down. He admits he did get upset when Naomi questioned him about his phone. He hasn't been knowing her long enough for her to be questioning him about anything. He figured it was best for him to remain quiet than to say exactly what was on his mind.

"You've been quiet for the past ten minutes Lawrence is everything ok?"

"Sure, I'm starving. I could use something good to eat right about now what about you beautiful?"

Naomi now had a smile back on her face. She was relieved she thought he was upset with her about earlier. She was most certain he had an attitude about the phone thing. "I would love something juicy and meaty, she replied with a sexy grin."

Lawrence eyes crossed from the thought of that response. He immediately got out of the car and opened the door for Naomi and then threw the keys to the valet. He kindly offered Naomi his arm as he ushered her into the building.

Once again Lawrence spared no expense. The place he brought her to was very upscale and beautiful. Naomi's eyes lit up when she walked through the doors and saw how amazing the décor and the atmosphere was. He had to smile because he knew he had done good.

*   *   *

Naomi's chocolate skin looked enticing in the glowing low light that was coming off the candles at the table. He found it extremely hard keeping his eyes off her. He's not even sure if he heard a word she said all night all he could do was stare at those juicy soft lips of hers the entire time. That soft pink gloss was making his mind go places it didn't need to go. At work blah, blah, blah, copier blah, blah, blah, was all he heard at least for the first fifteen minutes. "Did you hear what I just said? Lawrence? Lawrence?"

"Huh? He whispered softly. Yeah baby you said something?"

"Yes! I actually said a lot. Are you paying attention to me?"

"Yeah baby of course. What would make you ask me something like that?"

"I've called your name several times and all you were doing was staring off into space. Is there something on your mind?"

"Yeah you," he added with a sly smile.

"Hmm. Naomi added folding her arms. I bet."

"I'm serious. Ok, ok. I apologize for my actions but I can't help but think about how fine you're looking tonight. Not in a bad way though. (at least not this time he thought)."

"Ok Mr. I'll let that slide this time." She said while grabbing his hand. Lawrence stared at his hand for a minute. Moving a little too fast, aren't we? We've barely been here thirty minutes!

"Lawrence this place is incredible! She whispered. The décor is amazing. How did you find this place?""

"Nothing but the best for you baby."

"Aww you are so sweet. So, what do we have planned after this Mr.? I'm sure it has to be something equally as amazing as this."

Actually, I did but since this is only our first date I didn't think that was something she was down for doing. Then again, the vibes she's giving does have me a little curious. "I was thinking that after this we could take a drive up to the coast and take a nice stroll on the beach."

"Mmm that sounds really nice." Lawrence noticed Naomi started shifting in her seat. Maybe this date will end up the way he wanted after all.

A few minutes later they both ordered dinner and another bottle of expensive wine. Lawrence noticed that Naomi was drinking her wine a little way too fast, almost by the glass full.

"Whoa, whoa slow down baby. Don't you think you're drinking a little way too fast? I'm only on my second glass you're on your fourth."

"Aww baby I'm good. I have everything under control." Naomi could barely get her fifth glass up to her lips before Lawrence took the glass from her. "Ok I think you had enough."

"No, you're not my daddy. I said I'm good."

"Now, I'm sure you've had enough. I think it's time for us to go."

"Oh no. I was just enjoying myself. Besides I think this place is too beautiful to leave," she pouted.

"I'm sorry but you're drunk and we're leaving." Over Lawrence's shoulders he could see a couple of waiters whispering to themselves about Naomi's behavior. A few minutes later he seen one of them walking towards their direction. "Excuse me sir, but is the young lady alright."

"Sure, why wouldn't she be? Lawrence added clearly disturbed that he came to his table.

"Sir she looks as if she had way too much to drink. We just want to make sure you don't need us to bring your car around."

"Did I ask you to?"

"Um no sir. I just thought that maybe you wanted to leave to keep from disturbing the other customers."

"Look you!"

"Walter sir."

"Whatever your name is. I'm a paying customer like everyone else is and a very damn good paying one at that. Rather she had way too much to drink or not that frankly is none of your business, now is it?"

"No sir."

"How about you do me a favor. How about you ask them to pull my car around and get me my check will ya. While you're at it how about not expecting a tip. How does that grab ya?"

"Um yes sir. Coming right up Mr.?"

"Weldon!"

"Ok Mr. Weldon I'll be right back with your check."

"Thanks. Naomi, Naomi baby? We're getting ready to go. I think you need to wake up. Some cool air would do you good right about now."

"Oh no, shoot! Ok…. Let's go. Naomi got up to pick up her shoes. She bent over to pick them up. She must have forgotten that she had on thongs with her very short dress. When she bent over Lawrence noticed that the couple behind them faces turned beet red. He instantly ran over to cover her up with his jacket. All he could do was apologize to the couple and lie and say that she wasn't feeling well so he had to take her home. He picked up her heels and gently helped her up to her feet. When the waiter came back he paid the bill that came up to someone's two months' rent. Thank God, he had it like that. He snatched the card from the waiter's hand that probably thought he couldn't afford to pay it, gave him the eye and walked out the door.

They waited out the front a few more minutes for the valet to bring the car around. Naomi was so drunk she couldn't keep her hands off him. She kept kissing him on his cheeks and constantly clawing at his neck. He had to keep slapping her hands away to keep her from snatching his clothes off. He looked over at her and realized that going to the beach may not be an excellent idea. The best thing right now for them both was ending the date and taking her home. She was way too drunk to do anything else.

She should have told him before their first date that she couldn't handle her liquor. That's why you're supposed to get to know someone before you take them out first. Hell, she talked about everything else tonight but I see she fell to mention this major part about herself.

A few minutes later valet finally brought the car around. He had to forcefully snatch himself away from her to get her into the car. For her to be a small framed woman she was strong. He finally got her into the car but instead of jazz for the trip he cranked up some loud r&b instead. He looked over and a few minutes later she had fallen asleep.

He was a little upset but then again, he wasn't. He was more disappointed that the date had to end this way. He had put so much planning into this date he thought. He planned everything to the tea from the outfit on down to the shoes he would wear. Not to mention he had constantly listen to his two best friends many insults all day before the date even gotten started. Boy he's going to hate admitting to them that they were right after all.

Lawrence pulled up to Naomi's gate but realized he didn't have the code to get into inside. He looked over at her but she was sleeping so beautifully he hated to awaken her. But how else was he going to get her home. "Naomi baby I need you to wake up. He whispered I need your code in order for us to get inside."

All she kept doing was moaning and fanning him to back away. He waited a few more minutes and tried to waken her again. This time she slapped at his face trying to shoo him away as if she was shooing away a fly. He ducked just in time or she would've slapped him clean across the seat. "Dammit woman! Wake your ass up so I can take you in the house!" He yelled. After he yelled he had seen a car pass by. He then realized what type of neighborhood he was in . This wasn't the place to be causing scene.

There were security guards and way too many patrolmen driving around that place he'll be locked up before he knew it. He knew he had one last time to wake her up for the code or take her back to his place. Since she wasn't budging his place it was. After getting back into the car he sees it was now one thirty and way too late to call the girls to ask them what they thought. So, he guessed he had to handle this one on his own. He noticed that Veronica still hadn't called.

What's up with that? When was the las time she's gone that long without calling him? Was she having that much fun? Did she finally hook up with that Warren dude? Did she give him any he thought angrily? He shook his head forcefully trying not to entertain the thought while getting even more pissed off by the minute. He looked over at his date equally frustrated at her. How in the world does he get himself into mess like this over and over again? If he would only listen for once.

About forty-five minutes later he pulled into his drive way. Before he could put his car into park a huge smile came across his face. His phone finally buzzed.

CHAPTER 7

Where's the Party?

Veronica left the restaurant in a hurry. The further she gotten away from that place the better. She looked around for Warren and his family before she left but they were nowhere to be found. With all the commotion with her family going on she hadn't noticed that they had left. She was disappointed because she was hoping she would get a chance to talk to him again. Valerie had already pissed her off when she called him cute earlier. She knew she did it only to be funny but she refused to allow her within ten feet of him tonight at the fund raiser if possible she thought. That's all she needed was him making goo goo eyes with the lovely Val all night. She felt sick just thinking about it. All she could think about doing was taking a shower, changing her clothes and finally putting the past couple of hours behind her.

She finally reached her room. The rush of cool air felt good across her face. Although the sun was starting to set it was still extremely warm outside. The temperature was reading eighty-eight degrees and it was now six thirty. She knew she had to be dressed by a certain time but she needed to lay across her bed for a brief second. Veronica knew she couldn't tarry too long because she didn't feel like hearing her mom Debra's mouth about being late. She just needed a minute to wrap her mind around everything that happened today.

Veronica still couldn't believe she had met and came face to face with Warren Beasley. What was the chance of that ever happening again? Not to mention sharing a kiss. She knew it was only a kiss on the forehead, but it was still a kiss. She looked over at her luggage and realized that she hadn't unpacked a thing since she's been there. She might as well get up and get started now while she picks out her outfit tonight.

She still hadn't decided what to wear to the fundraiser. Hmm she thought, something cute but sexy, short, but not too short. Then again, I'm not old either so nothing extremely long neither. Black? White? Gold jewelry? Silver jewelry? Hmm…Veronica decided on a black scoop neck fitted knee length dress with the back cut out. She topped it off with black red bottom patent leather stilettos, a diamond necklace with matching dangling earrings. She curled her hair and pinned one side up to show off her sexy back. While she was putting the finishing touches on her hair she heard the front door and her sister came rushing in talking to the top of her lungs.

Veronica stared at the door for a second contemplating if she should slam the door closed. She wondered what could she be so excited about this time? Not to mention the fact that she was running late.

"Veronica? Where are you girlie?" Valerie screamed with excitement. Veronica immediately got up and slammed the door before Val came walking around the corner. Somehow that didn't stop her she still came rushing in the room. Something told me to lock that door she thought.

"Guess what? You wouldn't believe what just happened to me!"

"Try me," Veronica responded trying her best not to sound interested.

"Anyway. We just met Warren Beasley and his family."

"We?"

"Me, Mom and Dad. Well it was really dad. We found out that dad had already met him before, but he really introduced us this time. Girl why didn't you tell me Warren was that fine in person?"

"Really," Veronica snapped looking up at Valerie in the mirror.

Valerie ignored her gesture and continued talking. "Girl not only is he fine but he is such a gentleman. He kept complimenting me and telling me how beautiful I was. When I told him what I did for a living he said that he that he already he knew who I was. Can you believe that?"

Veronica slammed her makeup bag down on the dresser and walked out the room. That was all she could do to keep from strangling her sister to death. Who in the hell does she think she is? How dare her! She instantly stared massaging her temple because her head was killing her. Somehow she was starting to see her worst nightmare began to unfold right before her eyes. A second later Valerie comes rushing out of the room with a questionable look on her face. "Ok brat what in the world is wrong with you this time?"

"Are you kidding me Val? You're going to stand there and pretend like you don't know? You know what neva mind, don't even worry about."

"That's your problem you never want to talk about anything when it comes to me. I asked you a simple question. Why can't you act like an adult for once and give me a simple answer."

"Then I would be the only adult in the room."

"What!"

"Leave it alone Val, besides you wouldn't understand. So, let it go will ya!"

"No, I'm not! That's how we leave everything in this family. You stormed out of the room like I said something wrong or so horrible. So, I have the right to know what it was that I said that was so insulting. Is this about Warren again? You can't possibly be that obsessed?"

"You would like that, wouldn't you?"

"Like what Veronica?"

"Me saying I'm jealous of you and some guy liking you? Well I'm not so you can keep your enthusiasm. I have no reason to be jealous of you when it comes to anything especially when it come to a man. Let's make that VERY clear!"

"I can't tell or you wouldn't be carrying on like this over a simple conversation. You know what's so funny. It's the same ole mess over and over again. The same mess we've been arguing over since we were kids. Well I'm an adult now and I don't have to stand here and allow you to bully me just because you heard something that you didn't want to hear."

"Are you done," Veronica responded with no remorse. If so I'm running late. Your mother should be calling soon I'm sure."

Veronica walked off without another word. For the first time, she had gotten the best of Valerie. She didn't have her bull dog with her this time to back her up. It took everything in her not to slap her in the mouth to shut her the hell up. Who cares if Warren called her beautiful? She sees she couldn't wait to throw that in her face. I really hate her she wanted to scream clinching her fists.

She better stay as far away from me tonight as possible or she will regret it. If she's trying to make this a competition for Warren's attention then it's on sister! May the best damn woman win and I don't like losing.

Veronica finally calmed down enough to finish her makeup. A few minutes later she heard her sister's shower come on from her room. Good she thought that was her chance to sneak out without her knowing she was gone. She didn't want them to show up at the fundraiser together, she was still pissed off at her. She checked her phone she had ten missed messages. A few were from her mom who cares, one from her dad she'll see him at the gala, and one from Lawrence. She'll get back with him later also. He only wants to be noisy, besides he talks way too much and she's already running late as usual. She noticed she did have a missed call from an unknown number. She checked the time it read 5:30. She started to dial it back but realized that her time was already running short. Hmm who in the world could that be. Whoever it was they would have to wait until tomorrow.

Veronica grabbed her clutch bag sprinted for the front door when she heard Valerie's shower stop. She could hear Valerie running behind her screaming her name while the elevator was closing. She had no idea what she was saying and could really care less she thought. She wasn't sure how she would feel if she ran into Warren tonight. Boy Val sure knew how to ruin a near perfect moment. Up until now she had felt wonderful about her encounter this afternoon, now she doesn't know how to feel.

Now the only thing that was running through her head was Warren now feelin her sister. With her luck, it was a good chance that he was. She is a very beautiful and outgoing woman. There weren't too many times she hadn't seen Val leave an impression on any man she had encountered.

The elevator finally reached the main floor. The vestibule was still as busy as it was earlier. All eyes were on her as she walked down the stairs. She was receiving a lot of stares from all sort of men both young and old. After all she was looking very sexy in her dress tonight. She looked over right shoulder and seen her young handsome bell-boy from earlier. He was grinning from ear to ear when he noticed her looking at him. She just smiled gave him a cute little wave and a nod. He was fine she thought but way too young she had to keep reminding herself.

She asked the valet to bring her car around. She had rented a 2017 Mercedes S-class sedan for the week. There was no need of her staying in an expensive hotel and driving a rundown car. After all she was on vacation, so why not treat herself, she earned it.

While she was waiting for her car she noticed a nicely dressed couple about her parents age close by. She wasn't trying to be noisy on purpose but she couldn't help but listen to their conversation. She listened to how sweet the lady talked to her husband and how sweet he responded while the stood beside her also waiting on their car. When the car pulled up she noticed how gentle the man was with his wife and how he opened the door for her and how she said thank you to him with a smile before the door closed. She watched how they both drove off she guessed on a date deeply in love with each other. At least they seemed as if they were genuinely in love with one another.

If that had been her parents and her dad was trying to help her mom into the car the first thing she would've said was "Robert I don't need your help. I got it!" He would've just walked over to the other side like a sad puppy and got into the car. I'm sure they would've driven away in silence like usual. I often wondered if my daddy was really happy with my mom? I want to ask him so bad she questioned, but knew he wouldn't tell her the honest truth.

Finally, her car pulled up. She rushed off to the convention center as fast as she could. If she received one more call from her mom she was going to have a fit. There were so many times she could press ignore.

She knew there were going to be a lot of available bachelors and millionaires at this fundraiser. Being late for her mom was not an option for them. Veronica knew her mom weren't crazy about her but she did want to see her marry a very wealthy man. She was sure Debra already had the best men hand picked out for her favorite. Most likely the second picks or the left overs were all she had left for the picking.

*   *   *

Veronica's eyes widen when the doors open to the main ball room. She couldn't believe how many people turned out for her dad's event. There were celebrities from everywhere, her dad should raise a lot of money for sure. The amazing part of it all was that they were all there to support her father. I wonder is Warren here? He stated that he was coming, but what if he was too busy to attend? There were so many people in there it would be hard to spot him anywhere.

Veronica spotted her parents mingling at the front of the room by the stage. She made a bee line and headed that way. She could feel eyes on her as she walked by. She was looking very sexy and her black dress was defiantly on point. Her new designer Genni out did herself with this one. She told her recently if she kept that up that soon she would make head designer. If she keeps this up she will be on her way. Anybody was better than that Naomi. Thanks to Lawrence she'll be lucky if she will still be employed with the company after this weekend.

Her dad Richard greeted her with a biggest grin on his face. He looked incredibly handsome in his black tuxedo. Her mom better keep her eyes on him tonight before someone snatches him up. Her mom looked equally beautiful as well, but please explain why she had on a short black tight dress? With matching stilettos? That was out of the ordinary especially for her. Don't get me wrong it was cute, but who was she trying to impress? "Hi" Debra greeted with a fake smile.

"Hi mom," Veronica greeted her with a slight hug.

"You're late, she frowned. I asked you not to be late."

"I know mom, I had to get dressed. I don't see Val here either."

"It doesn't matter. I asked you to do one simple thing for your father and you couldn't even do that. I tell you Ronica you're just plain selfish."

"But ma?"

"But ma nothing. I don't want to hear it. Not now anyway young lady. We will discuss this later. Understand?"

"Debra not now."

"Ok Richard, this is your night. Get your daughter."

"Hey Peaches, you look absolutely gorgeous."

"Thanks dad and you look so handsome. So, have you met anyone new and young tonight?" she asked looking over at her mom.

"I didn't think that was funny."

"I wasn't laughing."

"Ok, cool it you two. And to answer your question no Ronica, no it wasn't like I was looking either Deb."

"Mm hmm."

"Changing the subject completely. How's everything going so far dad?

"Everything is going well so far. We just barely gotten started, you haven't missed much. The music just got started, we have food and drinks going around. So, drink up, mingle, take pictures, eat up enjoy yourself. Where's your sister?"

"I have no idea. I left her back at the room getting dressed. Like always she's taking her sweet time getting dressed."

"I see. Well I'm sure she'll be here shortly. Until then go enjoy yourself, when she arrives we will take our family photos."

"Ok dad sure thing."

Veronica was now feeling little better that she came out to the fundraiser. Before she had spoken to her father she wasn't too sure. The way her mom was coming across at her she felt like turning back around and going back to her room she already had one of the biggest headaches. She has seen a waiter coming by with champagne. Her and her mother reached for a glass at the same time. Debra snatched her glass away with an attitude. Veronica refused to turn around to give her the satisfaction of starting another argument. She'll be alright.

She walked off to check out the scenery like her dad recommended. Her mind was set on checking for Warren but just in case he hadn't showed up there were other very fine available bachelors there. She thought she spotted Warren from the corner of her eye a couple feet away from her. As a matter of fact, the closer the got she realized it was him. She tried to adjust her dress on the sneak tip before he spotted her. She wasn't sure if this was an appropriate time to approach him right now. She didn't want to seem too anxious.

Instead she made her way around the room to see who else was there. Veronica took pictures of and with as many celebrities that she could pose with. For once she could say she was actually enjoying herself mingling with the rich and famous. The music was dragging that wasn't like DJ Reality he was usually always on point. There was no way she was about let the music there suffer with all those people there. She knew she had to get to the DJ and ask him to switch the music up fast.

While she was walking up the DJ's booth she noticed her parents looked as if they were having a heated discussion. She saw her mom pointing her finger in her dad's face with tears in her eyes. She could over hear him begging her to calm down and get herself together. She snuck to the other side unnoticed to see if she could hear better what was being said. She then overheard Debra asking Richard why was he talking to that woman and who was that younger female she saw him talking to on the other side of the room? All Richard was doing was pleading and begging her to calm down and not cause a scene.

A few minutes had passed and he finally convinced her that she was the only woman that he loved and wanted to be with. That was all he had to say, somehow it worked. Next thing Veronica knew Debra went from being extremely angry to having this girl like attitude. It was vastly strange and weird to watch she thought. I tell you my dad has some serious talk game on him for a man his age. My mom on the other is seriously bipolar!

After they kissed and made up she got herself together like nothing ever happened, straightened up her clothes and walked out.

Veronica hurried out in the opposite direction hoping she wouldn't be seen. All the sudden she heard a loud uproar of oohs and ahhs coming from the crowd. Cameras were flashing out of control as the famous arrived. They had to be someone famous coming through for that type of commotion to be going caring on. Her mother suddenly appeared behind her "Who in world could that be I wonder?"

"I don't know. I'm standing here looking just like you are."

Next thing I knew here comes my older sister strutting thru the double doors looking like she came off the cover of Vogue magazine. I mean I can't take nothing away from her she looked jaw dropping gorgeous. All eyes were most defiantly on her this time even mine.

She was wearing this very long tight form fitting dress that fit her like a glove. I mean it was perfectly hitting every curve. Her make was light and flawless, she had her hair pinned up in soft loose curls hanging down her back. Once again, my mom went flying to be y her side. She wouldn't dare miss an opportunity for a photo op with her precious daughter.

They stood there for felt like hours taking photos. I'm not sure why I stood there and watched. Maybe it was out of discuss or maybe I was amazed how silly my mom looked caring on the way she did. I wondered did anyone else besides me notice this?

"Mom I'm sorry for being late. I got in late I had to shower and change my clothes. I had to have my makeup done. You know how it can be." She apologized.

"Oh baby, no problem we both understand. Besides you hadn't missed a thing we just barely got started," Debra stated.

Debra wouldn't dare turn to face Veronica. She knew her daughter had her lips ready to say something both mean and smart to counter the comment she had just made. Valerie noticed Warren walking in their direction and almost knocks Veronica down to get to him.

For what Veronica could see Valerie purposely gives him a huge hug and a big kiss on his cheek. From the look of things, you would have thought that they were dating or old friends. Wow! Exactly what did happen when they ran into each other this afternoon? Veronica tried to keep her composure trying to remind herself that she was there to support her dad not act a fool over some man.

She knew she had to get the hell out of there. She charged passed him and the whole stupid scenery. Before she could get away she felt a strong hand grab hers. "Excuse me but where are you going in such a hurry?"

"Excuse me," Veronica questioned snatching her hand away.

"So, you're going to rush passed me and not even speak?"

"Really Warren?"

"Yes really," Warren stated with a huge grin. Either this man is playing me or he's just plain stupid. Does he think I didn't just see him kiss my sister just then? What a joke. "I haven't seen you since I've spoken to you earlier. I was wondering where you had gotten to after you left the restaurant. I've called you earlier but you never returned my call."

"You called me?"

"Yeah about 5:30."

"Oh…yeah?" She had just remembered that she had a missed call round about that time that she didn't have time to answer. Had she known it was from him she would've taken the time out to do so.

"How did you get my number?"

"I got it from your dad. I remembered I had forgotten to ask you for it. So, when I've seen your dad earlier I knew he was the next best person to ask. You didn't mind did you."

"No of course not. "she responded now embarrassed.

She looked over at Valerie and all she could do was roll her eyes. She wanted to smile back and break out in a dance so bad but she knew that would be tasteless. She looked over at her mom who was standing now standing there with her arms folded and with mean look on her face. They both stood there looking at each other awkwardly for a second. After a second Warren suggested that they both take a walk outside alone to talk.

That sounded great she agreed. Anything to get away from those two. They both walked away silently out the back of the building. There was a bridge to walk on with a bridge located in the back with a bench to sit on. It had finally cooled off a bit so it was a nice evening to take a stroll. It was good to get away from the noise and the crowd for a minute as well. She was sure her dad and his people would be looking for them soon but they will be ok. They will only be gone for a minute.

She didn't know what to talk to him about this time. They seemed to have so much to share the first time around. "I didn't realize that Valerie was your sister. Somehow until now I hadn't made the connection. I knew you two had to be related but I wasn't thinking you were sisters."

"We don't look alike to you?"

"Actually no. I mean you favor yes but ones tall and the other's really short. I would've never thought you two had the same parents."

"Unfortunately, we do. Didn't you meet up with my dad this afternoon?"

"Yeah but they both weren't together. I met him and your mother first, then I was introduced to your sister by your mother."

"Really? I was told something entirely different. I was told that it was my father that introduced you two."

"No, I'm most certain it was your mom that introduced Valerie and I."

"Mm. Well it doesn't matter. So…what did you think?

"Meaning?"

"Do you like her?"

"If you're asking me do I like the idea of who she is no. If you're asking me if she's beautiful I can' lie to you. Yes, she is. She's a very beautiful woman."

What! Veronica felt herself getting light headed. She literally as if she was about to pass out. "Like I was saying she is a beautiful woman but after spending a few minutes with her I realized that she wasn't the type of woman I interested in or wanted to get to know."

"Mm," was all Veronica could mustard to say.   She   tried everything to fight back the smile that was trying to form on her face. If only Valerie could hear this she would scream. Serves her right. "Well what did happen when you two met?"

"Not trying to enclose any of my business because after all you two are sisters. I'm just going to say sometimes when you meet someone for the first time you know if you're meant to be right off bat. Not saying that I wanted to purpose or anything I'm just saying we just didn't click.

"I understand. So…what were your thoughts when you first met me?"

"Mm."

"Mm?"

"Let me finish," Warren added laughing. First of all, I thought you were very beautiful."

"Ok continue."

"Shaking his head Warren continued. "I liked the fact that you were the type of woman that weren't afraid to take chances."

"Really? What makes you say that?"

"The way that you were dressed. No other woman in their right mind would've worn anything that flashy nor showing that much skin."

Veronica suddenly felt a little embarrassed. Suddenly her outfit that she had chosen to wear earlier somehow hadn't sound like such a clever idea. Maybe her mom was right. Good thing she could get his attention or things could've gone completely wrong.

"You ok? Warren questioned. You've gotten quiet on me?"

"I'm fine actually. You may continue if you like."

"Sure, my pleasure. I also loved that right off top you were fun and easy to talk to. That doesn't always happen when you meet someone for the first time. From that second I said to myself that she was someone that I wouldn't mind seeing again and possibly getting to know further."

"Well Warren Beasley that sounds wonderful."

"You think so," he stated walking closer.

"I know so," Veronica replied. The closer he walked to her the more nervous she became. She just felt his intensions were to kiss her. She's been waiting and fantasizing for this moment for a long time. She couldn't believe that it was right before her. Before she knew it all she could feel was his soft lips touching hers. Her body froze for a second from disbelief, but she then quickly grasped what was going on and returned the favor. Their kiss lasted to her felt like for hours but realistically it was about two minutes. They both didn't seem to want to let go.

"There you two are! Veronica your mom has been looking for you everywhere! They need you to come take family photos asap!"

Whoever that woman was scared the heck out of them. They both had to laugh it off for a minute just to catch their breath.

"So, I guess I think we better get going huh?"

"Yeah, I guess so."

"Can we finish this later?"

"Sure," Veronica smiled.

Warren softly kissed her once again on the lips. Veronica quickly ran back inside before anyone else came out demanding that they were needed for something. When she made back inside she noticed that her family had already started taking photos without her. She didn't know what was all the uproar about if they had already gotten started.

"Hey Peaches, where in the world have you been? We've been looking everywhere for you."

"I was outside. I really needed to get some air."

"Already? But you just got here."

"I know dad. You wouldn't understand."

"Is everything ok?"

"It is now. "Veronica smiled.

"Ok. Well come on over here with us, Richard gestured with excitement. I need to have your beautiful face in these pictures with us."

Valerie was already on the stage posing like she was about to be on some cover of a magazine. "Um excuse me but if this is how the entire session is going to be I'll pass."

"Oh no, no, no. explain the photographer. We were taking their photos to past time. I do apologize I didn't mean to take up anyone's time. "Well you are," Veronica retorted rolling her eyes.

She tried waiting patiently for the photographer to finish. Warren suddenly walked through the door after being outside for about thirty minutes. I wonder why he was out there for so long she thought? Valerie noticed him also because her poses went from simple poses to being sexier and raunchier with each take. Veronica started to snatch her ass off the stage she was getting so upset. Instead of causing a scene she kindly walked over to the photographer and reminded him that her dad was paying him good money. If he wanted to continue to get paid that amount of money than he would get Valerie's crazy ass off the stage.

A minute later she saw Valerie and the photographer exchanging words. The next thing she knew Valerie was wrapping up her session and exiting the stage. She came by stomping down the steps by Veronica rolling her eyes. "I know you had something to do with what just happened."

"How you figure?"

"Don't worry about it. I just do."

"Ok ladies, Richard came running over. Are you ready?"

None of us were ready but we couldn't tell him that. If it wasn't for him none of us would even be there. We all one by one without even smiling walked up on stage. He was there excited grinning from ear to ear. Mom grabbed me by the arm forcefully "Don't you dare ruin this for him. Smile even if you don't mean it. Understand?"

I yanked my arm away and wanted to say speak for yourself but I just kept my mouth shut. How could I force a smile after that? And this is only day one. Are you kidding me?

*   *   *

Debra noticed that Richard was missing after the photoshoot. She had been doing good with keeping her eyes on him all night up until now. There were a lot of single young women there that would love to get their hands on her handsome rich husband. She asked around if anyone had seen her husband within the past ten minutes.

So, far no one had known where he wondered off to.

After the photoshoot, Veronica went to get a much need glass of champagne. She found that she loved being the center of attention tonight because she got to stand on stage and just watch what everyone was doing. She noticed that her mother Debra sneaking around as if she was looking for someone. She had a concerned look on her face like something was bothering her. She wanted so bad to ask what was going on but she was still upset with her for grabbing her arm earlier. She was sure she had a bruise.

Her dad was missing and nowhere to be found as well. What in the world is going on between the two of them she wondered. She watched as Debra sneaked off and disappeared into the back of the room. Without trying to be noticed she followed her. She looked over her shoulders to make sure her sister Valerie hadn't notice her sneaking around.

She wasn't paying her any attention she was too preoccupied by her favorite two things rich men. Veronica had to run to catch up with her mom. To be an older woman she sure moves pretty fast. She finally caught up with her around the corner still ducking and sneaking around. For some strange reason, she was trying not to be noticed. Veronica followed her mother for seemed like another five minutes up and down two more hallways. They reached the end of the final hallway she heard voices. It was her dad's voice and a lady's voice she had never heard before.

She couldn't make who the lady's voice was but whoever she was pissed her mother off. Her mother became instantly upset when she seen the two of them together. The next thing she knew she busted right in the middle of their conversation without hesitation. The lady had said a few words like she was trying to explain herself. My mom and her then exchanged words back and forth. I've seen my dad a couple of time trying to get in the middle to break them apart. After a few minutes of going back and forth the lady had enough and because of something my had said ran off crying.

I tried to get a glance of the woman as she passed by but all I've seen was a glance of her face. By her silhouette, she looked a lot like my mom just as beautiful but she had lighter colored hair. I stayed back in the shadow to make sure when she passed I wasn't noticed. When she left, I heard my mom screaming something at my dad about "You had no right inviting her here. Supposed she would've seen her."

Supposed who would've seen who? I thought. Then I've heard my dad say, "I didn't invite her she called me and said she wanted to come."

"So, you couldn't tell her no!"

"She's a grown woman Deb!"

"Dammit Robert! What kind of man are you? You told me that you're protect us."

"And I will keep my promise woman. Besides she said it's time she knew." It's time who knew what? Veronica questioned. Who was she? What kind of secrets are they keeping from us? Then she heard her mom scream "I'm her momma, I'll tell her when I'm good and damn ready. You understand me Richard? You no longer get to decide. "Next thing she seen her mom punching him in the chest crying like a baby. What in the world is going on? Should I even be watching this she questioned?

She stayed and watched them hold each other a few minutes longer and hurried back before she was noticed. Her head was spinning out of control from what she had just witnessed. Veronica had so many questions now going around in her head. Who was that mystery woman? Why did she look just like her mom? It could've been her sister. Mom said she only had one brother and that was Uncle Charles. She never said anything about anyone else like a cousin resembling her although her and that lady could go for twins! To be honest that lady looks just like me but older.

She wanted so bad to tell Val what she just witnessed but she had no idea how to explain it. Then again, she may not believe her. A couple minutes had passed and she seen her mom walking through the double doors. Like always she bounced back very quickly. You would've ever thought that she had been crying. Her hair, makeup, and clothes were all back in place like nothing had even happened.

A few minutes later her dad came walking through the doors with a bewildered look on his face. Now he on the other hand appeared as if his entire world was about to crumble. You could clearly tell that something was going on with him. He always had a problem with hiding his feelings. "Dad are you ok?" Veronica questioned with concern.

Her never said a word. He just kissed her softly on the forehead and disappeared out the front door. "Mom is dad ok?"

"He's fine, she snapped. Just fine."

"Ok…"

"He needs to just get himself together so he can make this speech and collect this check to complete this evening," Debra interjected.

Veronica turned to face her. She looked her over for a second. She had no sympathy for him in her face what so ever. It's like she was saying whatever hurt he was experiencing he deserved it. I for one couldn't stand seeing my dad like that.

"I'm going outside to make sure he's ok."

"Suit yourself. I don't care what you do," Debra responded with agitation.

Walking through the crowd my mind was a little cloudy. It has been years since we've been together as a family and in one day all it has been is drama. Could this day get any worse she asked?

She went all over the place looking for her dad. I was almost impossible to find him. I was almost like he didn't want to be found. After all that happened earlier who could blame him. She was getting exhausted walking around in those stiletto heels. She had better find him and fast or he was on his own. She seriously needed to sit down for a minute because she was starting to feel little light headed again.

The last place she chose to look was the balcony. When she got close to the door she could hear her dad talking like before. She was afraid to approach him because she didn't want to find her dad in the same predicament as last time or even worse.

When she reached the balcony her eyes nearly popped out of her head. She found her dad outside kissing that same woman from earlier. The very same woman that her mom a him were arguing over.

Veronica was frozen in her tracks. She was suffering from total disbelief. Her dad and another woman? How could this be? Who… is… this… woman? This… home… wrecker! She wanted so bad to interject but backed away instead in the shadows once again.

After they were done he hugged her, they exchanged a few words, he kissed her softly on the forehead and they both walked off. He went in one direction and she went in another. She was beginning to hate the thought of the forehead kiss. The meaning was really beginning to make her wonder. She did hear her dad call her name Marylyn. Marylyn? Doesn't even ring a bell.

When everything was, quiet Veronica broke down crying like a baby. She wasn't sure if it was from the shock of it all or disappointment. She felt a sharp pain shoot up the left side of her chest and rush up the back of her head. She was finding it extremely hard to breath. She had to sit on the floor with her back against the wall just to get herself together. All she was saying over and over was daddy why. What in the world is going on with you and mom and this mystery woman? She had stated in the past that she wanted her dad to leave her mom but not like this. If her mom knew what she had seen it would kill her. She couldn't stand her at times but she didn't deserve this.

She tried to stand to her feet before someone walked in on her. Her legs felt weak and wobbly as she stood. She made her way to the restroom to fix her clothes and makeup, after all she was her mother's daughter. There was no way she wanted to face her dad right now. Not like this

When she walked out the door the first face she was greeted by was Warrens. He greeted her with the most beautiful smile she could ever ask for. She really needed that from him right now. Hell, she could use a friendly anything to get over the hurt she was currently feeling.

"Hey beautiful, I've been looking all over for you. You sure are a hard woman to keep up with."

"I apologize, Veronica tried to smile, I had to take care of something important."

"Anything I can help with?"

"No. You are so sweet but everything is ok. I have it under control. (lying). Thanks for asking."

"Well I was looking for you because your dad is about to give his speech and they need you on stage."

"Really?"

"Veronica you sure you're ok?"

"Yes, Warren I'm fine. I will feel even better If I had someone as handsome as you escort me to the front of the stage."

"It would be my pleasure."

*   *   *

The applause was from the crowd was louder than normal when Veronica came walking through the door. Her head was now spinning out of control and she was finding it hard to focus with every step she took. The lights were all turned down except for the spotlight on stage where her family were currently located. Everyone were there waiting with smiles on their faces and extremely excited anticipating what was about to transpire.

Veronica wished that she could be just as excited but after all of the things she has just experienced and all of the things she had just heard; she didn't know how to feel. So far, the only highlight of the whole evening was seeing Warren's face again. When Valerie had seen Warren and Veronica arm and arm she was extremely envious of seeing them two together. How did that happen so fast, she questioned?

That's all she needed was for the tabloid to pick up on seeing them two as a couple. If that was to leak they could make it on the best couple list and no way was she about to allow that to happen. Nope no way was she was she having that. She had to break them apart and fast. Veronica wasn't even famous she doesn't even deserve a man like him. Enjoy your fun little sister while it lasts. It won't be happening long she laughed to herself.

Veronica walked on stage. Her head was now spinning faster than before from the bright lights. She could barely make out a word her father was saying as he took center stage. All she heard was loud clapping and could see was blurred visions of people standing around smiling. She could hear her mom suddenly asking her over and over was she alright. Nothing could seem to come out. It was like she was in a trance. She felt herself slowly drifting back. That was the last thing she remembered.

A few moments later she opened her eyes and seen her mom standing over her with tears in her eyes. Her dad was on the opposite side just standing there quietly rubbing her hand. She looked over her head Warren was standing there with a concerned look on his face. She couldn't believe that he was still there. After all that she put him through she just knew that he would be long gone. Not only that how in the world did she pass out. How embarrassing is that! My head is killing me she thought. She tried to getup but everyone gestured to lay back down.

People were still in the ball room but the crowd was starting to whittle down a bit. They were mostly standing around staring and whispering about what just happened. I've noticed my sister Valerie was standing to the side discussing something with someone over the phone. I guessed it must have been important because she kept waving her hands and arms in the air as she spoke. Warren finally took Veronica by the hand. Robert looked down at Warren holding Veronica's hand. He wanted to question what was going on but with what all that was going to on he opted to keep his mouth to himself for now.

"You gave us quit a scare for a minute. Warren stated. When I've saw, you hit the floor I didn't know what to do. Everyone thinks you should go to the doctors. I for one agree."

"No! I'm fine I just need some rest. This has been a really long day that's all." Veronica assured him squeezing his hand.

Debra looked at them both then at their hands she also had a puzzled look on her face. She had a "What did I miss?" questionable look on her face. They both chose not to say a word they remained silent for a minute. "I think I better go back to my room lay down and get rest up for tomorrow. I've been running full speed since I've gotten off the plane. I'm just tired."

"Ok Peaches if you're saying that's all it is ok. But once you get some rest and you're not feeling better in the morning; you're going to the doctors. You hear?"

"Sure Daddy. I hear you."

Veronica still couldn't force herself to give her daddy proper eye contact. She still wasn't sure exactly how it was she felt about him for that moment. Seeing her mom with tears in her eyes as she awakened was confusing enough already. Seeing her mom concerned period was confusing alone. She had to be drunk no change that she was drunk to be crying over her she chuckled.

Valerie came rushing over with that famous model strut of hers all in an uproar. "Great! Just great! Thanks to sleeping beauty it's a good chance all of this may end up on the internet tomorrow! So, thanks a lot!"

"Valerie is that all you think about? Yourself? Questioned Richard angrily. Your sister could've been serious injured!"

"Dad don't you understand this could hurt my career. It could even hurt your career!"

"I'm really disappointed in you young lady. Your priorities should be your family and the health of your sister not your career."

Valerie looked over at her family and at Warren. Everyone was looking at her almost with discuss on their faces. She really could careless she had her own life to live. She wasn't about to allow her family's nonsense to ruin it. She sure doesn't need Warren judging her.   "I'm sorry but I don't view me as being the selfish one here. I'm most certainly not going to say that I am and I'm not about to apologize for it."

"Now Val listen hear. I had abou…"

"No dad it's ok she's entitled to her own opinion. She's free to say whatever it is that she wants to say. It doesn't even matter at this point. Warren, would you please help me to my feet?"

Valerie just stood there with her arms folded across her waste with her back turned to everyone. She could've cared less if Veronica was hurt or not. All she's seen was her sister passed out on the floor in front of a lot of famous rich people and cameras at the biggest function of the year. They want her to apologize for being angry about something like that, well they all have another thought coming!

Veronica was greeted by strangers from all direction on her way out the door. All of them gave their sympathy and best wishes. Many seemed to genuinely concern as they wished her speedy recovery. Her dad gave her his now infamous forehead kiss and told her to keep him informed and to get plenty of rest. He promised that he would call and check on her in the morning.

Warren ensured Richard that she would get to her room safely. Richard gave him the side eye and told him to make sure that she makes it to her room alone. Veronica had to remind her dad that she was an adult and that she was old enough to make that decision. Besides after all she had seen from him tonight he had no right to judge nor tell anyone what to do. Just the visualization of him kissing that woman still made her sick on the stomach.

Debra was silent the remainder of the evening. She still looked as if she had a lot on her mind. The las thing she said to Veronica was goodnight. No smart words, no arguing, nothing. She was sure what happened earlier was weighing heavy on her shoulders. Poor mom she wanted her to know what her no good cheating husband was up to so bad. But how could she tell her without hurting her. Maybe she already knows. One thing she have found out about older women they know far more than what they lead us on to believe.

Maybe he has been doing this for years and she's been keeping it to herself. That could have a lot to do with her bitterness. But then again with her who knows she has been bitter for years. Hell, most her life. For that to happen they would have had to be raise up together Veronica had to smile to herself.

Just the fact that her mom showed her concern finally touched her heart. She knew if she ever mentioned it to her she would deny it. To think it had take me getting hurt for that woman to ramosely show she cares made her question a lot.

The valet brought Warren car around. He wouldn't allow Veronica to drive, he was too worried about her condition. He said he would get someone to drive her car back to the hotel for her. She thought that was very sweet of him like always. She still was having a tough time trying to figure out why was he being so nice. They both had just barely met that day. It was his weekend to shine, he clearly could be doing something or someone else. Why was he still there with her? He gently helped Veronica into the car. She watched him as he walked back to say goodnight.

He had a very strong presence around everyone she noticed. People seemed to look up to him, even older people. That was one trait that stood out and was making him look extremely attractive.

He kept looking back over his shoulders as if he was trying to see if she was looking at him. "Yeah", she said out loud, I see you cutie."

Like always she tried her best not to stare but this time she was finding it hard. The longer she was in his presence the more attractive he became. That had nothing to do with just his looks either.

She was still trying to wrap her head around the things that transpired tonight. She wished she had some clues about who was that mystery woman and why was she kissing her dad? Forget that why was she even there period? The main question of the night is why was her presence such a threat to her parents, especially her mom? So many questions but not enough answers.

Veronica watched her dad stand there acting as if he didn't have a real care in the world. How could the only real man she ever loved hurt me (us) so bad and not even know it. She was more angry than disappointed if anything. She would expect her mother to be a cheater before he would if you wanted to know the truth. Regardless I don't feel like even thinking about it anymore, the pain is just way too much.

Richard walks up and taps on the window as Warren got into the car. She didn't want to roll the window down but she made herself do it anyway. "Well Peaches you're in Warren's hands now. Once again get you some rest, now you hear me?"

"Yes daddy, for the last time ok. I'm not a baby I'm ok."

"I know baby. We're just concerned about you. You scared us back there."

"Daddy I promise you I'm fine," she tried to smile.

"Are you sure?"

"Yes, daddy I'm sure."

"Okay, just making sure I love you. Goodnight and thanks again Warren for taking care of our baby."

"No problem Mr. Martin it's my pleasure," he looked over with a huge grin. Veronica without hesitation smiled back.

She realized she hadn't said I love you back as she watched her dad walk back inside. For some reason, she couldn't at least not yet. They sat there for about five minutes before driving off. While they were pulling off they seen Valerie running outside the building screaming something and waving her arms. Once again, she couldn't make out what she was saying then again who really cared. It was getting late she was tired and her head was hurting. If it was that important that's what a cell phone is for. Until then she will talk to her tomorrow.

CHAPTER 8

Friends or Foe

"Goodnight Chasity"

"Goodnight."

"Goodnight lady, I really enjoyed you."

"Yeah same here (lying). Chasity stated trying her best to smile.

If one more person tells me goodnight I'm going to scream. I'm so ready to finally get out of this place I don't know what to do. This has been a long and drown out week. I'm glad to be almost finished with school to finally be working towards the career of my dreams. The one thing I cannot stand are these long drown out lectures and these boring professors.

I hate that I don't have anyone here to talk to but these boring tired wanna doctors. Most of them act as if they already know more than the professors that giving the lectures. They are all starting to get on my very last nerve. I must say I have learned a lot on this trip despite all the other nonsense, but I'm ready to get my behind back home. I miss my friends and family.

I still haven't found the nerve to call Lawrence and tell him my news. I'm sure he's pretty upset with me and thinks that I'm leaving him hanging. That was not my intension at all. This afternoon I had planned to tell him everything but no one told him to go ruin it with that "Please call Veronica" mess. I'm sick of that name coming out of his mouth. She's my girl and all but I rather it'll be me he talks about not her.

It's hard to believe Lawrence and I have been friends since fifth grade. The very first time I met him we were on the playground. He was just as cocky then at ten then he is now. I was climbing the monkey bars and he was staring at me from the other side of the fence. When I turned upside down I felt someone grab a handful of my booty. I immediately jumped down and slapped him across the face. He jumped back at me and asked me what was my problem? I bluntly informed him that my momma said that if somebody tried to feel my booty to slap them right in the face.

Then I informed him that if he ever tried that again that I will punch him in his stomach real hard the next time. From then on, he either took me seriously or thought I was crazy. Every day he was there waiting for me on the monkey bars with a candy bar as a gift. I wasn't studden him but I always took his candy bar.

He was so in love with me that when other boys would come over to play he would tell them that I was his girlfriend. That meant that they weren't allowed to play with me. Back then I never question him I just went with it. It pretty much stayed that way throughout the remainder of elementary school, high school and even into college. But when I got into high school other guys started noticing me so that's when I started pushing him away.

Everyone thought that I was crazy for dumping him as fine and talented he was. I knew he was fine, driven and destined to be great but my mind was settled on a man that wanted bigger and better things. I wanted to date older more experience guys. When I told him about my decision of course he was heartbroken, so was I when he left for college without saying goodbye.

We enrolled at the same college but when I finally attended he was already extremely popular on campus. It was almost like he had already forgotten about me. The same year we both met Veronica we were still dating off and on. That was after I apologized of course. He was so in love with me then he immediately gave in. Veronica never knew we dated at the time and I didn't intend for to either. Even now I don't think she would be able to handle it.

Between late night studying and the incredible sex everything was going great. Even then I told him that I preferred to remain friends because I was new at college. I wanted to get my feet wet at first. I didn't want to be tied down by just one person. Besides I wanted to check out the older single more established men on campus. Like before he couldn't handle it. Although I had hurt him it was easy to maintain his heart that was until Veronica came back a changed woman.

I mean she was absolutely gorgeous! He couldn't keep his eyes off her. He went from calling her homely, and hating her guts to falling deeply in love with her. That was the first time I had ever been jealous of any female when it came to him. Don't get me wrong Veronica and I became very close that year but Lawrence had always been mine. I never told her that I wanted to share him.

It has been hard playing pretend all of these years when we all get together knowing I didn't want him nowhere near her. Now I'm sure anyone would be able to clearly understand me if I told them why this news would kill our friendship. I'm sure if I told them the news suddenly they both would be like why now? I don't blame them. What could my response honestly be. Too afraid. Chicken. It doesn't matter all I know is that I want my man back and I'm willing to do whatever necessary to get him back.

Then on top of that he has the nerve to be out on a date with that huge breast big ass Naomi! He really gets my last nerves sometimes. I could use a drink. I wonder where's the closet bar? I want to get so drunk I won't remember a thing, then get laid by the first man that has a face.

Chasity went to take a much-needed shower. She was scrubbing her neck and chest while thinking about Lawrence and the times they would take hot steamy showers together. She could remember how sexy his body looked when the hot water would hit his smooth chocolate skin. Her body tensed up when she envisioned his strong hands going up and down her shoulders while his soft lips were kissing her neck. Missing his touch almost made her climax repeatedly in the shower. Before she completely lost control she stopped herself. She instantly went from excited to angry.

What was it about her that he no longer desired she questioned? Was she no longer enough for him? Was there sex or the many things she had done to him and for him no longer enough? A rage went through Chasity. She quickly climaxed and finished her shower. She decided that she would throw on the sexiest dress and heels she packed.

She had long mahogany brown hair that fell passed her shoulders, she thought that she would curl it up and let it hang. She then slipped on a red tube dress with matching six-inch open toe stilettoes. Panties or no panties? Hmm she laughed? No panties, she decided to take a pair and some wipes just in case she has an accident later.

She threw back a second shot of 1800 grabbed her purse and was out the door. Whatever there was to get into tonight she was down for it. She thought that she would first check out the bar located downstairs in the hotel. She wanted to see if there were any action popping there before she headed anywhere else. The 1800 had already starting to kick in and she was already feeling that famous warmth in her belly.

Chasity noticed three handsome middle aged men already sitting at the bar. At least one of them must be looking for some action tonight she thought. Instantly when she was about to walk through the door her phone started ringing. Just like clockwork it was Lawrence calling. He always seemed to call when she was in the mood to do something wicked or daring. It was like he knew she was up to no good. Not tonight she thought angrily. "FUCK YOU LAWRENCE" she screamed at her phone and then hit ignore. Not tonight joker enjoy your huge tits!

She stumbled to the bar and tried to flirt with the bar tender when she asked him for her first drink. Like always all eyes were on her. Chasity was a very attractive beautiful woman. That red dress was giving the men vibes that she wasn't only single but she was also very available. She made eye contact with the gentleman sitting next to her. She smiled at him and he smiled back. Ok she thought so far so good.

She received her drink winked at the bartender and tipped him then made her way over. "Hi" she almost she whispered she was so high.

"Hi yourself."

"So, you want to get out of here?"

"Whoa! Ok, why so direct?"

"That's the only way I know how to be baby."

"Well this is the type of gentleman I am. Hi my name is Chad Benoit," he stated extending his hand.

Chasity stared at his hand for a minute. You have to be kidding me right now she thought. I'm standing here looking absolutely tasty and I'm drunk and you want to shake my hand. Ok I'll play this game.

"Okay… a handshake how cute. Nice to meet you Chad it is? So, where you're from Chad?"

"New Orleans. Born and raised."

"You?"

"Me, what"

"Where are you from?"

"Hold up let me sit down before I answer any questions, and if you must know I'm from Charlotte, NC. What brings you to Orlando? Business presume?"

"Not all business. I do try to enjoy myself every chance I get."

"That's nice to hear."

"So, what brings you here if you don't mind me asking?"

"I'm in school to be a surgeon, and we had to come here for a lot of hands on things and a bunch of lectures for a week."

"Impressive!"

"Why?"

"I mean it's not often a man runs into a female doctor. Let alone a surgeon. I'm really impressed."

"Yeah yeah. Chad!" Chasity tried everything in the world to keep from falling off the stool. Since she was now tipsy she was finding it hard to remain focused. This is one time she can truly say she had way too much to drink. It wasn't her plans to get that drunk but the more she thought about Lawrence's feelings for her or the lack there of she needed something strong. Drowning herself in her sorrows was the best thing to do to help get passed the pain that she was feeling. Then again, she was sitting beside this handsome Chad maybe he could help ease her pain.

"So, Chad how long you said you were here for?"

"I didn't."

"Oh?"

"But if you must know I'm here for at least two more days that is unless I have a reason to be here longer."

"And why might that be?"

"I don't know you tell me."

"Hmm you're funny Chad Benoit. Really funny," Chasity taking a huge gulp of her drink.

"What did I say that was so funny?" He frowned when he seen how much alcohol Chasity was trying to consume at one time. He figured something terrible had to be going on with her. He was sure it had to do with whoever that Lawrence dude was he heard her yell out earlier.

"I barely know you. I'm drunk as a skunk and you're trying to tell me that you actually find me attractive? Yeah right."

"I never said I agreed nor disagreed to that statement."

Chasity immediately stopped drinking and gave Chad a long "Are you kidding me" stare. Chad just sat there with this reassurance look on his face.

"Men like you make me sick!"

"Excuse me?"

"You heard me. Men like you make me sick. You think you're slick, don't you? Sitting over there smiling I see you. Sitting over there smiling like you know you gone get some. Well you're right. You just might. Chad!"

"That hadn't even crossed my mind. I was just enjoying my drink and this mmhmm interesting conversation. Ms.?"

"Simms", Chasity responded never looking up from her drink.

"Ok Ms. Simms explain to me why you're so drunk at only 8:30 in the evening?"

"It's complicated you wouldn't understand."

"Try me."

"Nope Chad! Not sure if I can trust you. Don't know you like that Chad!"

"Why do you keep calling my name like I've either offended you or I owe you money?"

"I like the sound of it. No, no wait answer me this Chad! Why do men mistreat women that they know are in love with them?"

"This wouldn't have nothing to do with someone named Lawrence would it."

"What business of yours if it does? Just answer the question Chad!"

"Ok Ms. Simms my question for you is have you told him how you felt?"

"Not exactly."

"Then there you have it. How can you expect for him to run to you with open arms if he doesn't know that you have feelings for him?"

"Well Chad! I feel as if he should already know. We have been best friends since the fifth grade. We've dated off and on since college why wouldn't he know."

"What no Chad!"

"Whatever Chad!"

"Well to respond to that Ms. Simms! Honestly there's no way he could possibly know how you feel. You stated that you two were friend since fifth grade correct?"

"That's what I said Chad!"

"Ok…Anyway, although you have dated when you've gotten older and I'm sure messed around. Since you never showed interest in him that way nor showed that you want to develop a relationship. In his mind, he pretty much decided that he should move on and I'm sure you both left it as just that."

"Meaning"

"Meaning over the years he only kept things the way you liked it, on a friendship basis."

"So, you're saying it's my fault?"

"I'm not saying it's anybody's fault. It's just how you both allowed your relationship to be."

Chasity sat there and tried to think about things for a minute. She didn't want to admit it but Chad was right. She had all but made sure things over the years never gotten too serious between her and Lawrence. If he got too close she would on purpose push him away. In the past, it would hurt his feelings, sometimes even made him cry. Most of the time she was always nonchalant about it almost like she carried less. Now the tables have turned he's moved on and she don't know how to take it. Boy I tell you karma is something.

"You ok? You gotten quiet on me?"

"Yeah Chad! I'm good… just thinking. Chasity lets out a big sigh. Just thinking."

"Look I know we didn't get off to a good start and I know you don't know me. But honestly you look like you could use some air."

"You're absolutely right Chad! I don't know you. Me going somewhere with you may not be an excellent idea."

"I was only suggesting a walk on the strip, in the light with lots of people around. I will even let you lean on my shoulders until you sober up."

"That actually sounds good. Chad you're not that bad after all. So far!"

"What I no longer owe you money?"

"Don't push it Chad!"

"Ok now we're back."

Chad gently helped Chasity off the stool. She fault hard to stand on her feet. Chad noticed that she was having a tough time standing and walking. He then sat her back down walked out the door then came back with a pair black slippers from the souvenir shop.

Why is he being so nice Chasity questioned? He doesn't even know me. I'm drunk probably look a mess by now. I have no idea how my breath smells by now. Not to mention that this man is gorgeous and rich. He clearly could be with anyone of his picking. Why in the world is he wasting time with me?

"Okay give me your feet."

"What are you doing? Chad!"

"Woman give me your feet!"

Chasity hesitated for a second then decided to give in. She thought this was weird on so many levels, but what hell just go along with it she reasoned. Chad carefully removed each heel and gently put on each slipper. The cushion felt so good to her toes. She didn't want to admit it although her shoes were cute and expensive they were killing her feet.

This time Chasity stood but she remembered that she chose to not wear panties. She thought for a minute that she should say something. But she didn't know what type of woman he would've thought she was to be out in the open that way. Then she felt like telling him never mind and just go back to her room and just sleep it off. Then again, she may not ever see a man this rich and fine ever.

"You ready?"

Looking up she smiled for the first time. "Sure I might as well be."

*   *   *

Veronica finally made it back to her hotel room. Her head was now throbbing like crazy. She wanted to lay down to block out the questions she had going around in mind. Before she did that she really needed to take something for her headache first. Warren volunteered to walk her up to her room to make sure she was ok. Even though she was kind of hoping he would she was now nervous that he did. They both walked off the elevator straight to the door in silence.

Her hands were sweating and shaking so bad she could barely get the key in the door. Warren noticed how bad her hands were trembling and offered to open the door himself. This was one time she really needed to take her Ditropan for her hyperhidrosis. She most certainly didn't need to be sweating all over the place out of nervousness.

Veronica smiled nervously at Warren and thanked him for coming to her rescue once again tonight. When they were finally inside the first thing she did was flop down on the nice plush coach. The softness from instantly helped her start to relax. She laid back and closed her eyes for a second and enjoyed the quietness. They had forgot to turn the lights on but it was ok because the lights from the city made the atmosphere very calming. Warren brought her a glass of orange juice and some Motrin. He was always on time she noticed, never skipping a beat. There's no way this man could be real.

She took her pills. Afterwards allowing her head to sink as deep into the pillow as possible. A few minutes later she felt Warren's warm arm lifted her head. The warmth of his shoulders relaxed her even more. She wanted to wrap every part of him around her and just lay back and sleep on his chest. In the quiet she could hear his strong heartbeat. She had almost forgotten how wonderful his cologne smelled from the first time she had met him. She leaned her nose over deeper into his chest to get a better whiff of his sweet scent. She promised herself as long as she lived that she wouldn't ever forget that scent.

They both laid there quiet for at least thirty minutes. She must had dosed off for a second because the sound of his cell phone startled them both. They both looked around and realized it was Warren's that was ringing. He talked to whoever it was very briefly. It was almost like he was trying to rush them off the phone. It was now five minutes until midnight. Warren must have forgotten he had a tournament tomorrow Veronica was thinking. He has no business still being here.

"Why are you still here Mr.?"

"Excuse me?"

"I asked why are you still here. I'm fine, you have a very busy day ahead of you tomorrow. Go home!"

"Yeah I do and I'll leave when I'm good and ready. Not a minute sooner," he said with a warm smile.

"Warren I'm just saying you've done so much for me already tonight. I would feel awful if you shot a terrible round because of me."

"Look what I've done for you I done because I wanted to and I would do it again. Besides I will get enough rest. So, you can stop worrying."

"I'm not saying I don't appreciate you, I just don't want you to be tired that's all."

"Are you trying to get rid of me?"

"No, it's nothing like that."

"Are you having company over?"

"Now Warren stop it! And no."

"Then why are we having this conversation? Is something wrong?"

"No."

"You're sure?"

"Yeah I'm sure (lying). Veronica couldn't admit to him that she was nervous as hell. Now that they were both finally rested they were both also alone. What do they do? What do they talk about? She never pictured things getting this far with him. Ok Veronica it's time to put your big girl drawls on. What if this could be it? What do I supposed to do she thought nervously? Why are they so many questions!

"Veronica you ok?" Warren asked with a silly look on his face. I guessed he noticed her talking to herself she chuckled. "Huh? Um yeah. Yeah. I'm cool. Cool," she responded obvious now nervous.

"Maybe I should go. It's obvious I'm making you uncomfortable."

"No! No, you don't have to leave. I meant I don't want you to leave."

"Are you sure?"

"Yes, I'm sure."

Warren walks back over to Veronica. Suddenly in the darkness she felt his warm lips touching hers. All she could hear was the sound of their hearts that was now beating out of control. He slowly lowered her down on the couch never removing her lips from his. Everything seemed to fade away while she was kissing him. If this how it was going to be she couldn't wait to see what happens next.

She wanted so bad to rip off his clothes and take him right there but she didn't want to seem easy. She was on with allowing him to take control. Suddenly the conversation she and Lawrence had come rushing back to mind. She was trying to be careful not to take it that far at least not yet but there was no way she was about to let go of his lips either. The longer they kissed the deeper the kiss gotten and the closer they were. The sound of his moaning was seriously doing something to her hormones. She knows she said she didn't want it to go further but he was making it very hard. She noticed that her moans were starting to get into rhythm with his. Next thing she knew his jacket and shirt was off. Somehow her dress was now at her waist and her bra was now off. Usually she would be embarrassed but not tonight.

Things were getting hot and heavy. Her hormones were all over the place as she thought about how bad she now wanted this man. She felt Warren stand up. She heard him pull something out of his pocket then she heard plastic rip. Oh, my goodness that's a condemn she thought! Ok now this is really happening. Next, she felt his warm hand pulling down her panties, she was even more nervous but there was no holding back now. They both tried foreplay for about four minutes. Then she felt his hands pulling her legs apart, then she felt what felt like his manhood touch the softness of her vagina.

Then he paused. "What?" He tried again this time it really hurt way more than the first time. It took everything to keep from screaming.

"Veronica?"

"Yes?"

"If I ask you something would you be honest with me?

"Mm Hmm."

"Have you ever done this before?"

"Meaning."

"Veronica are you still a virgin?"

Every part of me wanted to fall right through the couch or just simply lie. How in the world could he possibly know that she was she questioned? Did she have a sign that said "Warning, warning. She has not used it. It's too tight do not enter!" I mean really! "To answer your question Warren…yes…I am…a virgin." Kill me now!

Warren slowly backed away and softly kissed her knees. He then perceived to put his clothes back on. What in the? "Wait what, I mean what's going on?"

"I'm going home Veronica it's getting late."

"Okay care to explain?" When she went to go turn on the lights she turned around Warren was already fully dressed. He smiled walked over and gave Veronica the sweetest good-bye kiss on the lips. He paused for a second looked down at her and simply said "Not like this." Gave her a wink then walked out the door. Before he closed he said he'll call her later. "Not like this," Veronica mouthed while picking up her clothes.

She hurried and showered before Valerie returned. That saying was weighing heavy on her mind while she was in the shower. Along with all the other things that has happened her mind was now really a wreck. Was Warren saying that there will be another time? Was he saying he couldn't handle her being a virgin? What did that saying mean! She screamed.

She fell back on her bed rob on and all still dripping with water. The one time she needed to talk to Chasity she was not available. She knew Lawrence was on his stupid date so she knew no way was he available. During times like this she wished she had a sister she could confine in and share things with. But she guessed that was also out of the question. Oh well this time she would just have to suffer alone. How things go wrong so fast she pouted. Life is so weird.

Just then she heard Valerie strut through the door making a lot of noise as normal. Now she sees why she stays alone. No way in this world could anyone put up with that much noise this time of night. It would literally drive me crazy. Veronica was now both hungry and thirsty. She remembered that her dad had the fridge nicely stocked with their favorite things, but there was one problem Valerie was still in there.

She tried waiting her out but Valerie was lingering for a long time. Maybe she was eating herself she reasoned. Finally, with anticipation she said the heck with it her stomach was now starting to make angry noises. Veronica walked into the kitchen and her sister Valerie was there in her Pjs eating a turkey sandwich, grapes and drinking a juice. Even in Pjs and no makeup she was still gorgeous. "Hey you. You're feeling better?"

"A little. Just hungry now. I don't remember eating at the party. Thanks for asking me if I wanted anything."

"Oh well you're eating now. Me either. When I got here I was starving."

"Crazy night huh?"

"Tell me about it."

"You think mom and dad are ok? A lot happened after you had left."

"Mm really?" Veronica responded staring off into space.

"Are you ok Ronica?"

"Yes Valerie. Veronica snapped rolling her eyes. I've noticed a lot literally going on between those two."

"Like what? What are you getting at Veronica?"

"It's nothing."

"It's has to be something or you would've brought it up."

"Just let it go will ya. Dang it!"

"I knew that terrible temper of yours was going to reemerge sooner or later."

"It's not that ok. I've seen a lot of crazy and bizarre things tonight. I'm not going to say anything until I further look into it. If I say anything to you about it now, believe me it wouldn't make any sense. Now does that sound better?"

"I guess. Just promise me that when you find out anything you'll keep me informed."

"As bad as I want to say no, I guess so."

They both sat at the counter in silence eating their turkey sandwiches and grapes. It was now two thirty in the morning when Veronica received a text message. It was so late she started not to answer it thinking it couldn't be nobody but Lawrence. He probably wanted to chat about his ole nasty date he had. Like she could care less about what them two done and how many time they've done it. Nasty!

She opened the text and couldn't help but smile it was from Warren:

Hey beautiful ☺. I hope I didn't wake you. If so I apologize. I hope you're getting enough rest.

I wanted to say it was nice to meet you once again. Funny lol it's only been one day. I most of all would like to apologize for how quickly I walked out on you. When I stated, "Not like this" I was implying that I didn't want your first time to be like a one night stand.

There will be another time and believe me it will be a night you sure won't forget. ☺ Sleep tight and I will talk to you later.

P.S. I take it back. If I have a bad round it will be your fault. My hormones are a mess!

Veronica couldn't help but to laugh out loud. She now felt a lot better about what happened earlier as well. She was also glad that Warren was proving Lawrence wrong minute by minute. Although there was no way that she was going to tell him about what happened she frowned.

"What was all of that about questioned Veronica? I knew it had to be Lawrence sending you a text this time of night. He's the only man I know in their right mind that would be texting you."

"If you must know this time you're wrong. It was not from Lawrence."

"Then who was it from?"

"Wouldn't you like to know."

"It better not be from Warren. You know he asked me out to dinner?"

"What? Valerie please."

"He did after when we were introduced. Before I left he said why don't we get together sometimes and I said sure."

"That's what most people say after meeting someone and he sure didn't act that way last night at the fundraiser."

"You can believe it or not that's all up to you. I just know he did."

Could she really be telling the truth? Well rather she was or wasn't. It was time she finally put a stop to her sister's competitive nonsense.

*　　*　　*

Lawrence woke up to the worst headache he had in years. For some strange reason he couldn't remember anything that happened after he got home last night. The last thing he could remember was receiving a phone call around one thirty. He remembered he was excited about answering the call because he thought it was Veronica finally calling him back. He just knew it was her calling to share how her first day was in Texas. Come to find out it was only one of his homies asking how did his date go. After he cussed him out for one calling him so late, two calling him period, and three for calling a man and worrying about what the hell he did on his date.

We are not females. We don't be sitting around sharing shit. I told him that he was the most simple minded person I've ever seen. I'm sure I said much more that I would have to apologize for whenever I see him. We're boys hopefully he didn't take me too seriously. If he did fuckem.

He sat up on the edge of his bed and rubbed his eyes. He then took a long hard look around his room that was a complete mess. What in the world happened in here he wondered? He can see they got drunk because he could see several beer and wine bottles strolled all over the floor. He can't remember the last time he has seen his place looking a mess like this.

Not only that he couldn't remember where in the world he had taken Naomi. All he knew he didn't take her home because they couldn't get inside due to the code situation. A second later he was stopped in the middle of his yawn by a loud moan. "What the hell? Naomi? You're still here? Awe damn so I didn't take you home."

"Good morning giant," she whispered.

"Giant? he probed. Now I have heard of tiger, and maybe even slugger. But GIANT?"

"I wasn't talking to you exactly, I was referring to him," Naomi stated pointing at his Johnson."

Lawrence stood up and snatched the covers realizing that he didn't have any clothes on. You did it again Lawrence he thought out loud. You just had to prove the girls right. If they could see you now they both would be singing in unison "We told you so." There's nothing worse than proving those two right. I have to get her the hell out of here and I mean now. Then I'm going to call the cleaning lady to come to clean this mess.

"Come back to bed baby it's still early."

"Um no. Uh I have a lot of things to do today."

"So, that's how you're going to treat your fiancé now?"

"Huh? Fiancé? Girl aint got no fiancé. Gone on with that trouble."

"Baby you don't remember giving me this, this morning," Naomi reminded him showing him her very large diamond ring. Lawrence almost choked on his saliva trying to speak. "What's that?"

"The very expensive ring you bought me right before we got back to your place. You remember after we came back from seeing that man with the pills."

"Girl what pills?"

"The pills I was telling you about that I sometimes get from this man that helps me relax."

"Hold up wait. I know damn well I didn't take no pills from an unknown person?"

"Uh huh."

"What in the world have I gotten myself into! He yelled.

"I need for you to calm that down."

"Look yo…" Lawrence had to cut himself off because he felt some serious anger rising. Fiancé', pill popping? Veronica is going to kill me! I have to find a way to get out of this mess before she gets home.

What type of woman is Naomi? Is she trying to get me killed? Not only that who in the world was this mystery man and what type of pills were they? I really don't remember a thing.

I still don't care if I'm supposed to be engaged to Naomi or not she still has to go! I need to clear my head. I can't tell right now if I'm coming or going. On top of that I'm pissed because I'm yet to hear from Veronica.

Lawrence wasn't ever known as the type of man that would beat around the bush. He knew he had to tell Naomi exactly what was on his mind. "Ok Naomi my place is a mess and I need to get myself together. I could use a nice hot shower right about now. You have two choices: You could either shower with me and afterwards go get us breakfast. Then I'll take you home after my cleaning lady leaves, or you can simply take your ass home by uber. Those are your only two choices.

"Thanks for giving me so many options."

"Well… come on. I don't have all day."

"Then I guess I better choose number one and choose to play with giant again huh?"

"That's up to you, he stated rolling his eyes. Hurry up woman!"

"You're so pushy babe."

"Yeah, yeah."

About forty-five minutes had passed before they finished showering. Naomi was fully dressed and out getting breakfast and the cleaning lady was finally on her way. Lawrence was prepared to give her a serious tip because his place was a mess. He was almost embarrassed to let her come in to clean. Oh well that's what she gets paid for.

Lawrence lived in a beautiful large one bedroom loft overlooking the city in Charlotte, NC. He loves sitting at the table in front of his huge picture window to do all his office work on his computer. He loved eating and drinking healthy like most people now and days so instead of coffee in the morning he opted on herbal tea. Like most of the world he always checked his messages and read his time line to see what he missed from the night before. One of his friends tagged him to a video from some fundraiser that read "Sister of famous Model passes out". He almost fell out of his seat when he realized who it was. He couldn't get to his phone fast enough.

He was now surpassed pissed. Not only did Veronica not call him last night, but she didn't have the decency to call and tell me about this. He had to find out this news from someone on the internet. He looked closer at the video. "Oh, now I see why she hadn't bothered to call me. Old boy Warren was rubbing her hand while she was laying down!"

Lawrence angrily tries to phone Veronica. Just as he thought it goes straight to voice mail. Damn! He tries a second time again it goes straight to voice mail. This time he leaves a message. "Ok sleeping beauty I see you have your phone turned off that's fine. Seen you passed out all on the net. When you get, this message call me back! Later!"

I see she can sit there holding hands with him but can't call me back and tell me something that important. I see how you want to be Ms. Martin and you still better be a virgin!

Lawrence stood and started pacing the floor. The more he paced the angrier he became. A few minutes later Naomi came back with breakfast. He barely even noticed that she had walked back into the room. She didn't say a word she calmly placed their food on the table exactly the way he liked it. After all she has been getting his breakfast and lunch for the past eight months. She knew better to ask him if he was ok. Everyone knows how he gets whenever he's upset about something. Naomi glanced up at him he was still pacing. Without a word, she continued doing what she was doing.

"Oh, what's up. I just noticed you were back."

"Yes, baby I've been back. Why don't you come sit down and eat your breakfast Naomi suggested," glancing at the computer screen?

"No, I'm fine. I got too much on my mind right now."

"BABY! I said come sit down and eat! Besides she stated calmly, I can't have people saying I don't feed my man."

"Lawrence noticed the sudden change in Naomi's voice. He never heard her use that demanding tone before. He started to say something to her but in a way, he was way too upset to care. If it should happen again he will be sure to correct it.

He hesitated for a minute more then he walked over and took his seat. It was almost eleven thirty and he was passed hungry. He couldn't wait to hear from Veronica to give her a piece of his mind.

He noticed while they were eating that Naomi kept staring at him and looking over his shoulders at the computer screen. He didn't put two and two together at the time but he sure he would later. He caught her at times with a weird look on her face as if she had something to ask him. "Is there something wrong Naomi?"

"No. Not at all," she said with a blank response.

"You're sure? I mean now is the time to get it out in the open."

"No, babe I'm good."

"Ok. This is your final chance to say what's on your mind. I'm not giving you another chance."

"Honestly Lawrence I'm good."

"Ok suit yourself."

"Have you calmed down yet?"

"I'm as calm as I gonna get. Why?"

"Mm ok."

"Anything else you need to know?"

"No. I guess not."

"You got your things together and ready to go?"

"Yeah! Can I at least finish my breakfast first?"

"Sure take your damn time," he responded angrily pushing his food away. What in the hell is her problem? He wiped his mouth and excused himself to his room without a word. The cleaning lady was finally done with his room. Everything was once again spotless. He loved that woman. She had been with him for four years now. If she wasn't so old he would date her. Except they probably wouldn't have sex and she wouldn't be able to talk only clean. He was tired of hearing females say anything for the past couple of days.

He has one friend he's in love with that acts like she doesn't know he exists, one he has sex with on the regular that's acting weird and one that's in the kitchen he's supposedly engaged to. He still doesn't know how in the hell that happened, that's driving him nuts! Everything is nuts right now.

I'm glad it's a lovely day out it would be nice to go out and shoot some hoops. I don't feel like being around anymore females right now. Later is a different story. I can either apologize to Naomi to ensure that my night will go easy or say forget it take her home mad and call someone else. Either way I'm going to enjoy my evening he thought. I can't wrap my mind around this engagement thing. What was I thinking?

A second later he hears the door open and Naomi appears into the room. She walks over and grabs him by the waste. "I'm sorry baby."

"What?"

"I said I apologize."

"For what? Woman what in the world are you up to?"

"For my nasty attitude. I know I can be difficult sometimes baby. I just want you to know that it won't happen again."

"Okay…"

A moment later Lawrence felt Naomi's huge breast on his chest and her mouth was swallowing his lips. She was attacking him like she had never kissed him before. He was pleased and confused all at the same time. This was not the same woman he left in the Livingroom he was thinking. His phone all the sudden started buzzing. He looked down it was Veronica's number. Finally, he thought. Naomi looked down at his phone and looked back up at him. She instantly snatched the phone and hit ignore. What she then put on him made his lips and toes curl. Let's just say he never spoke to Veronica.

*　*　*

The walk Chasity had to admit was helping her to clear her head. This time she hates to admit it but she had way too much to drink. For the first time in a while felt embarrassed to even admit it. She had this fine ass man Chad with her that she barely knows trying to help take care of her drunk behind. Then she has the nerve to keep bringing up another man. One that doesn't even care about her at that. Go figure!

"You're quiet."

"Yeah, the cool breeze feels good on my face. Chad!"

"Okay, so now you're awake. I never seen anyone actually sleep walk before."

"Funny Chad! I wasn't sleep walking I was thinking. Trying to get my head together."

"Look like to me you were deep in thought. Care to share?"

"Why should you care."

"What again no Chad? That's twice tonight."

"What you're keeping count? And no, I'm not that upset with you right now."

"Oh, so my name only sounds like you got your finger stuck in the socket when you're upset is what you're saying? Got it!"

"Or maybe when I'm really drunk. Either one or the other." Chasity stated laughing.

"You know what. You have a beautiful smile. I'm not just saying it just to be saying it you really do."

"Well thank you…Chad. It's nice to finally receive an honest compliment for once."

"Mm, I see you're awake and ready to talk now."

"Not really, I haven't changed my mind about that. So, far I think you're a cool guy. I'm not sure about what's your agenda, but you're cool."

"Who said that I had an agenda? Why when a man's trying to be nice to a woman he has to have an agenda?"

"Well Chad, that's not our fault. If more men were as direct as you are presenting yourself to be then we wouldn't have a problem trusting you more. Even if we didn't trust you at the beginning it at least could make it easier later."

"I understand, and I actually don't disagree. Mm Ms. Simms you maybe on to something."

"Yeah, yeah. Enough mushy stuff. Right now, I just want to finish my walk, clear my mind and enjoy the rest of my scenery. If that's alright with you Chad!"

"Yes, ma'am no problem. I can deal with that."

They both took a quiet stroll up to the dock. Chasity was still amazed at how rude she was acting towards this very handsome and so far, pleasant man. The question is why was he still there? She know she had been nothing but difficult since the first time they've laid eyes on one another. If she had common sense she would forget about Lawrence and just concentrate on this handsome tall man before her. She could always save the news she was planning to tell her so called best friend for another time.

Let him continue to hold on to and remain in love with Veronica. Who cares about the love he proclaims for her really? The more she tried to shake the feelings she had for him the stronger they became. Who was she trying to convenience of these lies herself? The more she thought about all the time they spent together and how each moment was a lie the angrier she gotten.

"You know what I can't do this!" Chasity stormed off.

"Hold up wait. Do what? Chad asked confused.

"This, she shouted with tears burning in her eyes. Me pretending like nothing's wrong. Look Chad Benja, Boneunet, however you pronounce your last name."

"It's Benoit."

"Whatever, look I can't lead you on and have you thinking you're going to get laid tonight. To be honest you're not. I'm drunk because I'm pissed off at a man that I'm madly in love with that barely knows I'm alive. It's not because he doesn't know who I am it's because I let him go. He was madly in love with me once and I pushed him away. Now the shoe is on the other foot and want him back and he has since moved on. The worst part of it all is that he's my best friend, and he's in love with someone else. She also happens to be both of our best friend. I have been drinking all day because I have been too afraid of calling him and telling him how I truly feel. I chickened out half way through it now I don't know what to do. Go ahead and say, I'm a horrible person."

"No, I wouldn't say you're horrible at all."

"Then what would you call me?"

"Human."

"Ok…That's it?"

"Yeah that's it. You didn't ask me for advice."

"Well I'm asking you now."

"Ok, if you must know this is my opinion only. I think you fell in love out of convenience."

"What? What does that supposed to mean Chad!"

"How long have you known?"

"Lawrence."

"Ok, how long have you known Lawrence?"

"Since fifth grade so what."

"How many people have you both dated since then? Seriously dated?"

"Me…maybe two. Him honestly other than me one."

"How would you know exactly how many women he's dated seriously?"

"He told me. We share everything."

"That's another problem for you two to be sharing everything and not being married. But that's another story all together. Ok, he's the only man you have spent time with throughout your adolescent years, teenage years, and your adult life."

"Meaning."

"Meaning for as long as you can remember when you couldn't find a date, a boyfriend, a companion or needed to have sex he was the only man you depended on to fulfil all of those needs. So now that you're in a rut again who is it that you run to. See you falsely put way too much dependence on one man. So now you're upset with him because he's not available when you want him to be available. Now that you are you expect him to be there. You're more in love with the idea of who he was then not who he is now."

"You know what I'm not going to sit here and listen to this nonsense."

"You don't have to Chasity, but who to say that it's not true. When are you going to let, him go and live your life?"

"How about I let go of you now. Good night Chad!" The nerve of him. I didn't ask him to act like he was that doctor/therapist that comes on TV. I didn't ask him for all this advice. I just simply asked him to answer one question and he comes up with this mess. Well he can keep that so-called advice. I don't need it!

"Chasity wait! I can walk back with you. You don't need to be walking back alone."

"No, that's ok I got it. Unless you're giving me advice on which directions I need to take back to my room I'm good." Chasity yelled half way down the strip"

"You know what woman you're a piece of work," Chad yelled back.

"Yeah, yeah whatever Chad! Whatever." A few moments later Chasity hears footsteps coming up from behind her. Before she could turn to address him, she felt the softest pair of lips sweep across hers. "What are you doing?" she could barely whisper.

"Did you think I was going to let you leave just like that?"

"You are impossible. I don't even know you. How dare you kiss me like that."

"I can stop if you like?"

"Yes. No. Maybe, I don't know Chad."

"Make up your mind baby. Would you rather kissing me or would you like to continue fantasizing about a man that shows no interest in you?"

"Chad, I just met you. I barely know your last name. You could be married with kids as far as I know. Hell, you could be a rapist or killer"

"I promise you I am none of thee above."

"What is up with you? If you're supposedly this handsome rich man who can have any woman he wants. Why are you here with me?"

"I never said I was any of those things you did. All I said is that I wanted to be given the chance to further get to know this beautiful woman presented before me."

"Why do you want to do that you just met me?

"That's what I'm trying to figure out. Why even though I just met you I'm I so damn attracted to you. Minus the bad temper of course. Although I admit it was cute at times."

"Stop it you're making me laugh."

"There's that beautiful smile again. If I continue to make you smile than I know I'm doing my job."

"Is that so Chad!"

"It could be Chasity!"

"So, what now?"

"There's no what. I'm getting ready to go. Didn't you say you were on your way back to your room. Well woman get the walking."

"Ha, ha funny," Chasity stated bursting out laughing.

"No, I'm just kidding. I was hoping to enjoy the remainder of our evening. You feel like taking a flight?"

"Huh? What?"

"I wanted to get away for a couple of hours. I promise to bring you back. I think," Chad smiled.

"Where are we going and can I even trust you?"

"Well let's see. I'm about to board my Yacht and go straight to the airport. You are on foot alone, in the dark about five miles from the hotel. You can either come with me or you can take the chance walking back to your room alone. That ma'am would be that way." He stated pointing in the opposite direction.

Chasity stared at Chad for a minute. She then looked passed him down the street that was now extremely dark and filled with strangers that she didn't know. Should she take a chance on this man she questioned? This is where she missed talking to Veronica. If things were like it used to be she would've had her answer on the spot with just one phone call. Then they both would laugh about her response, she sure it would've been something like "Girl hell yeah I would go are you crazy. If you don't I will. Shoot, tell him to come get me!" Then we both would be hollering about it.

Of course, I knew I would have to call her later with the details. Now because of me and my pettiness I have no friends to share this moment with. I have to make this decision on my own. Oh well.

"Well Chad! I would love to accompany you on your trip."

"Yes! I mean that's nice to hear. Bring those lips here woman."

"Whoa wait now! I do have a few stipulations. At any point, you even act like you want to go crazy I don't have any problem pushing your ass off your own plane. Sometimes I don't know what "no" means, so I better not hear it often that way you won't.

"Ok I promise I won't try to die early, and I was hoping you would say the second part," Chad mentioned with a huge grin.

"Ok I'm ready whenever you are. Just let call my best friend Veronica…and…tell her…where…"

"What was that baby?"

"Nothing Chad. It was nothing just old habits. Just…old…habits."

CHAPTER 9

How Can You Spell Relief?

Veronica tossed and turned all night. She couldn't shake the nightmare of all the things going on in her head from the night before. She immediately jumped out of the covers in a cold sweat. She now realized it was morning. She looked over at her phone on the nightstand it was reading six-thirty. I think I dreamed all night she thought staring up at the ceiling. Tossing and turning constantly with no ending. Waking up in cold sweats felt like every five minutes. One minute my dreams were pleasant about Warren. The next I was stuck in a terrible nightmare.

I couldn't shake the vision of my dad and that mystery woman kissing. She was always the recurring monster in my dreams. She kept appearing trying to take me from my mother's arms. My mom fought hard, but she would come right back. At times my mom would break down crying in defeat when the lady Marylyn finally took me away. Somehow my dad seemed to always be in the center of it all. It was the weirdest thing. Funny I always thought that the monster would be my mom if I ever had a nightmare like that. But not this time.

My dad the glue. Well the one I always thought was the glue that kept our family together. Should have been my protector in my dreams, but whenever I needed him he was nowhere to be found. All of this had me waking up with a terrible headache like I've had since

146

yesterday. I'm not sure if it's from the fall or from all the excitement last night. Maybe I do need to see a doctor.

Great more missed calls Veronica shouted looking down at the phone. I see I have one message from Lawrence and none from Chasity go figure. Let's see what Mr. Weldon has to say about his date last night like I care. "Ok sleeping beauty I see you have your phone turned off that's fine. Seen you passed out all on the net. When you get this message call me back. Later!

"Great…" she thought. Dang it. With all that's been going on I just remembered I had forgotten to call those him and Chasity to tell them about the fall. Now they had to find out through other sources. Great! Just great! Now I know that I will never hear the end of it. I see he left more messages. I'm sure he's real pissed. Let me see what it was he seen that has him so upset.

Veronica pulled up the browser and typed her name. To her surprise her name popped up instantly. Wow! I guess I am a little popular. But she got pissed when she read the title. "Sister of famous Super Model passed out". Really now? Is that right? The only reason I'm trending is because of Valerie? What kind of mess is that! She almost closed out the silly video but chose to look at it anyway.

She opened it and scanned it closely she smiled when she seen her family standing around looking concerned. All except Valerie. Look at her carrying on looking silly. Just plain embarrassing. She was still surprised by Debra's actions. She was not prepared to see her convey any emotions. Seeing Warren by her side rubbing her hand was priceless. That alone could be why she was trending, everyone is probably trying to figure out who she is. Oh yeah that could be the reason Lawrence is so pissed off. I know how much of a fan he is of Warren's. Not! Well I'm not calling him back right now.

Veronica froze the picture to get a better look at things. She noticed that her mother had a weird look on her face and was staring at the door as if she was staring at something or someone. She widened the screen to see if she could get a better look to see what it was that had her mother's attention. She noticed in the left corner of the screen was the same mystery lady Marylyn standing at the door. She thought she was asked to leave. Why was she still there?

"Ok sleepy head I need you to get dressed. We have to get going." Chimed in Valerie what seemed like out of nowhere.

Immediately Veronica slammed her laptop closed. She didn't want Valerie to know what was going on yet. She still had way too many questions. "I'm about to get dressed in a minute, and happy birthday old lady," Veronica yelled back.

"Thanks! And I'm not old just wiser. What were you watching just then? Valerie questioned. Please don't tell me it was that God-awful video of you from last night. I'm still trying to live that down."

"You're trying to live it down! Valerie, you are hopeless some-times you know that. "

"Whatever. Do you know how many phone calls I've received since last night? Do you know how any times I had to explain to people what happened? Then on top of that I had to fight trying to keep my name out of the tabloids"

"No not at all Valerie please explain. I was the one that fell and hit my head but I'm sure all of that talking must have been hard on your supermodel brain!"

"Funny really funny Ronica, but you would never understand."

"You're right and I don't care to. Have you heard from our parents?"

"Yes, earlier. Dad called and said that we are going to have a later day than planned due to him and mom had a late night."

"Oh? Why was that?"

"That's what it was I had to tell you last night when I got in. That was until you caught that bad attitude as usual."

"Val when I walked in here last night you were stuffing your face with a turkey sandwich. You never said a word about anything else," Veronica responded very dry shaking her head.

"Whatever I had my mind other things, she corresponded. That's why I was flagging you down when you and Warren was driving off. Apparently, some mysterious woman appeared out of nowhere and started screaming at mom "Why didn't you tell her? You had your chance! Next thing I knew I've seen our little momma charging at this woman full speed like a bull."

"What? I can't believe it!"

"Believe it! It took dad and two body guards to pull mom off this woman."

"Wow! What in the world?"

"I know! I thought the entire scene was both crazy and bizarre. I for one have no idea why all of this even happened. No one is telling me a thing. I asked both mom and dad who she was they both ignored me as if I hadn't even asked a thing. I thank God the media was already gone. At least I've dodged that bullet."

"Shut up will ya. Wow poor mom."

"After it was all over mom just broke down and started crying like a baby. That could be why dad said they had a long evening."

"I can imagine. That makes twice she's broken down crying like that."

"What? Really? When? Why are you just now telling me about this?

"Never mind. Forget I even mentioned it."

"No, Veronica tell me. What is going on? This family just has way too many secrets."

"You're telling me."

"Anyway, Veronica everything about last night was strange. That woman looked just like mom they ***can go for twins!*** they both said in unison. Except this woman had light colored hair. So Ronica you seen this woman?

"Yeah just like you last night. The weirdest this about Val is that mom told us that she hadn't any sisters. Only one brother."

"I know that's why it's so hard to fathom why they look exactly alike."

"Not only that, but the real question is why mom hates this woman so much?"

"How do you know they hate each other?"

"Huh?"

"How would you know that they hate each other Ronica you weren't even there while they were arguing so how would you know that? What are you keeping from me? I want to know and I want to know now!"

"Look Valerie I don't know no more than you do (lying). When I find out anything I will let you know I promise. Right now, I must get dressed. It's already seven-thirty."

"I know you're not telling the truth, but I'm not going to keep pressing the issue. I'm going to call them to make sure they're doing ok."

"Alright you do that." Although she was upset about her mom and dad situation she had to call her best friend Chaz to tell her about last night. There was no way she was keeping all that juiciness to herself. No way Chasity was going to believe this she wanted scream excitedly! She ran back to her room to retrieve her phone. "Please, please answer this phone girl!" she giggled. Ok it's ringing.

"Hello?"

"Eww you sound like your breath stink."

"Ha ha forget you! And good morning to you too."

"Where are you heffa? Sure, don't sound like you're back at your room."

"I am in my room."

"Oh, sounds like your night went better than mine. Ooh do tell," Veronica stated grinning.

"Heffa why are calling me so early in the morning? At... hold up...seven thirty in the morning!"

"Yeah so."

"What is it Veronica? You better be calling me to say you've finally got some calling me this early. Or your ass better not be a virgin two times over. Meaning he flipped you over while having sex two times. Now which ones was it?

"Well... almost."

"Almost! You called me this early for an almost! A possibility! Girl bye, I'm going back to bed. I could really use a couple of hours more of sleep."

"Sounds like you had a rough night hoe. Where were you at and who were in you?"

"Look, you have one more time to call me a hoe, Chaz stated laughing and if you must know I spent my night talking with my legs closed. They weren't almost opened like someone else's I know, and you called me the hoe."

"Ha ha. I need your behind to next time shut the heck up and simply get some then I wouldn't have to deal with you being so damn cranky so early."

"Whatever. So, did this almost half sex happen?"

"I'm not telling you nothing else with your mean self."

"I be doggone! You're going to tell something. You called and woke me up so you're going to spill your beans woman."

"Ok! With your mean behind. Well, we almost did it but he stopped."

"Why? Chaz whispered. Why are we whispering, she asked?"

"I kind of don't want Valerie to hear us."

"Seriously?"

"Chasity come on now!"

"You two sisters get on my last nerve, but continue."

"Anyway, we stopped because he noticed that I was a virgin."

"What! How in the hell was that even possible Ronica?"

"He said he noticed how tight I was."

"Is he the Vagina police now? Girl something is strange about that. Let me guess afterwards he jumped up and leaves."

"Well yeah. How you know?"

"That's what they all do. Girl I told you to be careful. They are all dogs. Rich, poor, thugs, wanna bees, gay straight it doesn't matter these days."

"But hold up. He did text me later to apologize for walking out the way he did and stated that he wanted to get together at a later time."

"To have sex I'm assuming."

"Chaz, he didn't say that."

"He didn't have to but I'm sure that's what he meant. You're a big girl though aint that's what you're always saying? You can make your own decisions. Remember once you give it away you can't get it back. It don't come with a return receipt hun."

"I know that. I've given it a lot of thought Chaz."

"You're sure about that? You barely know this man. He's just someone you've had a crush on but willing to give our jewel away to. But you make your own decisions. Remember no return receipts!"

"Will you stop saying it like that."

"I'm just making sure you hear me that's all. Do you know how many of us wished we could go back to where you are now and stay there! You are blessed and just don't realize it. I say wait until you know you're ready."

"Anyway heffer, right now I would rather explore my options than be cranky like you," Veronica joked. She was trying her best to ignore everything Chasity just said to her a minute ago about being careful with her decision. Up until now she realized she really hadn't thought about carefully at all.

"You're funny you know that."

"Really huh, so what's his name?"

"Who said he had a name?"

"Chaz?"

"Ok…it's Chad and that's all I'm giving you."

"So, what's he like?"

"That's all I'm telling you."

"That's not fair Chaz! I told you everything about Warren."

"That's your fault, besides you talk too much. But I love you anyway."

"Whatever heffer! Keep yo secrets. Love you too."

"Well I'm sleepy yo ass is just way too chipper for me this morning. Call me back and we can talk more about your almost leg splitter later."

"Forget you."

"Uh huh. Later."

"Bye girl."

"Bye!"

Shoot! Veronica thought I still forgot to mention to her about me passing out. I see she fell to mention it also. It was if she hadn't even known. I have to call her back and tell her before Lawrence does. When he's upset he makes a huge deal out of everything. Let me just call her back right quick. "You have reached the phone of

Chasity. I'm sorry I'm not available at this time. Please leave your name number and a brief message I'll promise to get back with you at my earliest convenience." Dang it! Just as I thought.

Veronica finally got dressed. She was more excited now to get out and enjoy her day than ever. She felt she needed to clear her head after hearing all the news she heard this morning. What Valerie told about her mom and the talk she had with Chaz concerning her virginity her headache wouldn't seem to leave.

Richard kept his word and wanted to play a family round of miniature golf this morning at the country club. Veronica was down with it but she was hoping to see Warren again instead. After breakfast, they met at the golf course. She hoped everyone will be acting their normal selves as usual like last night never happened.

Veronica picked one day to dress like everyone else and wore her favorite pink polo with a white mini skirt. To be different she chose to opt out and wear pink shoes instead of white; with yellow and pink socks. Plain was just not part of her description.

She was looking forward to her mom and sister being dressed just like her. But when she walked around the corner onto the greens she seen those two laughing it up with a very handsome instructor. They wore two very short miniskirts and sleeveless halters that tied around the neck. If she wasn't awake she either would've thought she was still suck in a nightmare or in the twilight zone!

"Oh, hi you finally made it darling," Debra greeted her smiling.

Yup it's official I'm in the twilight zone Veronica thought! "What…in the…world is going on with you two? What are you wearing?"

"Baby what are you saying you know I dress like this all the time," Debra stated giggle like a school girl.

"Ok who are you, and what have you done with my REAL mom?"

"Oh, Veronica lighten up and have some fun. We're here to learn how to play golf. So, this very handsome instructor decided to teach us."

"Hi I'm Aaron Barnhill. Nice to meet you," he stated extending his hand.

"I'm sure you are, Veronica stared at his hand. Where's my dad?"

"Veronica stop being so rude and shake the man's hand."

"I asked where's my dad?"

"Girl's he'll be here shortly," Debra responded in her regular voice. Now shake the man hand."

"Nice to meet you Mr. Barnhill."

"I'm not my father you can call me Aaron," he stated smiling.

"No, Mr. Barnhill is just fine."

"Okay…Suit yourself. If you like we can go ahead and get started or do you prefer to wait on Mr. Martin."

"I prefer to wait," snapped Veronica.

"No, I think we should get started. What about you baby?"

"Sure, why not mom. No need to keep this handsome gentleman waiting."

"Ok then let's get started. Everyone grab your clubs."

Next thing Veronica sees her mom and sister run over to their clubs and acting as if they were the two most helpless women on earth. It was sickening to watch. They were both bending all over moaning saying "Please Mr. Instructure could you use your big strong muscles to carry our bags. We're just too weak and helpless to carry our own." Where's a nice tornado when you needed one Veronica was thinking. This is getting to be passed embarrassing. What in the hell did I really walk into. Why were they both dressed like this? Better yet why was my mom even dressed like this and flirting openly with the golf instructor! I wonder if what's going on had anything to do with what happened last night? Did she know about what happened between dad and that Marylyn woman?

If not she sure acts like it. If not then her ass is just plain acting crazy as usual. Veronica decided that now was the best time if any to call her dad. He needed to get down there and fast. She couldn't understand why he was missing in action, after all he was the one that planned the day for them. Just as she thought voice mail. Does anyone answer one their phones anymore she questioned? She tried again great! She got him this time. "Hey dad! Where are you? We are all here waiting on you."

"Hey Peaches. I will be right there. Something important came up. I've taken care of it and I should be there no later than five or ten minutes. Is everything ok?"

"What could be more important than spending time with us? Um you asked was everything ok, I'll let you judge that yourself when you get here."

"I'm not understanding baby. Peaches are you ok? I've noticed that you've had an attitude with me ever since last evening."

"No dad, I'm good (lying). I was just upset at the fact that you weren't here. After all you did plan this day, I thought you would at least been the first one here."

"I understand. Like I said something out of my control came up, but regardless I'm on my way. Should be there in a bit."

"Please hurry. I can't be the only one here to experience the mess that's going on here."

"You're losing me again Peaches."

"Dad all I can say is that you'll see it for yourself when you get here."

"Ok baby girl, see you in a bit."

"Ok dad." Veronica found it hard watching her mother and sister carrying on the way they were with that instructor. They act as if she weren't even there. Wait until her dad finally gets here she wanted to shout so bad. She couldn't wait until he seen what his wife had on around this man. There's no way you could tell me he seen her before they departed this morning. If he did she had to switched and changed her clothes after they left each other. Veronica most defiantly wants him to see the way the instructor has his hands all over her for himself. She was sure he knew he weren't paying a full day for that!

After speaking with her dad just then, Veronica was still stuck on last night. She made a mental note to call her Uncle Charles to ask him about the mystery woman Marylyn. If they have any additional family member or missing family she was sure he would know. The last time she had spoken to him he was retired divorced and living on Virginia Beach. It should be easy to travel to see him if need be to retrieve more information.

She just need to make sure to get right on it. Veronica walked back out to her mother and sister to see what they now were up to. Just as she thought, they were still up to the same nonsense. She checked her phone to get the start time for Warren's round today. She had texted him earlier to wish him good luck and to let him know that she will surely see him later. He responded with an ok and a wink. That was short and sweet but was ok with her. She knows he was trying to stay focused for his round today.

She wasn't trying to sound selfish but she was glad when all of this was over so she could get to where he was. "Well hello there she heard a strong voice over her shoulders. So, how's everything's going so far."

"Hi daddy, Veronica greeted him kissing Richard on the cheek. Take a look for yourself." She was angry with her dad but she still loved him. She couldn't dare judge him too much until she got down to the bottom of what was going on. Even if it meant sneaking around asking questions.

"I see a lot has been going on. Hi Debra, Valerie. What's going on here." he questioned as he walked up to the greens.

"Hi Mr. Martin, the instructor extended his hands. A wonderful day we're having huh?"

"Save it! I'll get to you later. Deb what in the hell do you both have on?"

"What these old things. They are just clothes honey, Debra commented. Are you angry?"

"Damn right I'm angry. No, scratch that I'm pissed. What are you trying to do woman?"

"Nothing Hun. Isn't this how you like things," she responded continuously smiling.

"This is not the time nor place for this Deb."

"Have it your way Richard. After all you always does."

"Mom and dad what is going on?" Valerie questioned. This is not the place for this."

"Young lady you don't have the right to question me about anything with the way you are dressed."

"Dad I am a model. I wear stuff like this all the time."

"It doesn't make it acceptable for today."

"I'm a grown woman, I can wear what I want to ware."

"You watch your tone when you talk to me young lady. I am not your mother."

Valerie's lips were pressed so tight you would've thought she had just eaten a lemon she was so mad. At the same time, she knew not to say another word. I can't remember the last time I have seen dad this upset. Mom was also unusually tight lip as well. I sat back and watched it all quietly. I didn't want my dad chewing my head off.

"Now you two have the nerve to be dressed like this today after belittling your sister/daughter for what she had on yesterday. At least what she had on was tasteful and she was covered up." Yes daddy! Veronica wanted to holler out.

"I don't know what to tell you Richard. I mean do you want us to go change?"

"The way I'm feeling now it would be for the best. No way am I going anywhere else with you two dressed like this. As for you, pointing at the instructor, I paid you to teach us how to play golf. Not to fondle all over my wife and daughter. You can consider your tip loosed for today. Understand!"

"Yes sir. I hear you loud and clear."

"No, I don't think that's not fair dad!"

"Valerie, you dare to have something to say to me right now?"

"I'm just saying. Aaron I'm so sorry."

"It's ok. I understand. I'm good."

"Yeah there's no need apologizing to Mr. Muscle Man he's good. Have a lovely day Mr. Muscle Man."

"Um yeah. On that note. Nice meeting you all. Have a nice day." he responded walking away.

"Yeah, bye Mr. Muscle Man," Veronica smiled waving."

Valerie looked back and forth at her mom then at her dad and stormed off behind Mr. Muscle Man I meant Aaron. "Richard why did you have to do that?"

"I suggest you do the same Deb. Veronica and I the ones with normal clothes will be doing some site seeing while you two get redressed. We will meet you in one hour downtown. I'm giving you only one hour that's it. Understand?"

"Sure, whatever you say Richard."

"Give me some sugar woman." Debra without hesitation gave him a kiss and without another word walked off back to the hotel to get dressed.

All of this was really confusing to Veronica. It was all like night and day. One minute it was like her mom was in control, the next it was like her dad was telling her what to do. She just knows she needs to stay as far out of it as she could. All she wanted was questions from last night and nothing more.

"Ok… Everything about that was weird. Please tell me you thought so."

"Ah yeah, Richard commented with a chuckle. Like you normally would say, what in the world did I just run into?"

"Dad I have no idea. Do you think it had anything to do with what happened last night? I had a talk with Valerie and she told me about what happened after I left."

"Where are you getting at? Before I even answer that I can treat you to your favorite milkshake or ice cream your choice."

"Cool, ice cream sounds wonderful. Now answer my question please."

"Are asking about that woman she was arguing with that may have something to do with it."

"Who was she dad?"

"Who was who"

"That lady dad. Who was she?"

"That's nothing for you nor Valerie to be concerned about you hear."

"But dad she attacked our mom. Shouldn't we be concerned?"

"Concerning that part yes, but everything else you let me worry about that. It's nothing me and your mother can't handle."

"I beg to differ. She was fighting last night as old as she is. Then today she comes out here dressed like a video vixen. So, don't tell me that's having it under control."

"Peaches you have my word when I say I have it. Have I ever steered you wrong in the past?"

"Well no." she responded. Until now really what she wanted to say. She was getting nowhere talking to her dad. The more she questioned him the more he would beat around the bush. Looked like Uncle Charles would be her best bet so far. When it came to her he never kept anything to himself. He always told her everything. She hasn't seen him now in almost three years. She hoped this time things will be the same as they were in the past.

*　　*　　*

During their down time while Veronica's dad was inside the parlor getting ice cream she finally returned Lawrence's call. She realized she hadn't talked to him since she left home. She was sure he must be passed upset with her by now.

"Hello." Veronica heard on the other end.

"Why does it sound like you're dragging?"

"Why should you care? I haven't heard from you since you left. I see you're having fun."

"Ok… I see you're upset with me. I will take that, and I'm calling to apologize for not calling you since I've left. No that's not like me to not talk to you for an entire day. I also want to apologize for not calling you to tell you about me passing out last night. It's not that I didn't want to, it's that I was so tired when I got home I went straight to bed." (well almost).

"Sure, you did."

"Sure, I did what?"

"Neva mind, I guess I will except your ole sorry apology after two hole days."

"Lawrence it's only been one day."

"Well Ronica it feels like two. So, how's the family?"

"Everyone is ok I guess."

"Why did you say it like that?"

"So much has happened in these two little days, I wished I had the time to tell you about it all."

"Why you don't? What are you up to now?"

"Well mm hmm, me and dad are out site seeing and getting ice cream. While the other two has been ushered back to the room to change clothes."

"Huh, I'm not following you."

"Well dad had planned a day of miniature golf for the family. When we get here the Duchess and her counterpart were both dressed like they were in a Luke video."

"What! Why the hell. Why weren't I there to see that."

"Anyway, you sleaze. When dad got, there and seen how the instructor was fumbling all over them and how they were bent all over in front of him with those short skirts on he went off. He immediately demanded that they go back to the room to change clothes. So, while they are there we are spending time together."

"Wow! That is crazy. I tell you what there is never a boring time around your family."

"Tell me about it."

"What brought this on. I never heard of your mom carrying on like this."

"I don't know Lawrence. Maybe it had something to do with what happened last night at the end of the fundraiser."

"Well damn! What happened then?"

"Well mom got into a fight with some mystery women over God knows what."

"A fight. Momma? Seriously? What in the world is going on with her. Shoot, maybe I should've came. This sounds like my kind of vacation. Full of drama!"

"Shut up will ya!"

"Well who is this mystery lady?"

"We don't know dummy that's why she's called a mystery."

"Funny Ronica, very funny."

"All we know is that she looks just mom but has light colored hair like Valerie's."

"That's strange, because you said mom didn't have a sister. Only one brother Uncle Charles."

"I know that's why this is getting weirder by the minute. I tried beating around the bush and asking dad about it. But of course, he didn't tell me anything."

"Oh, you weren't getting any answers out of him. You know older people are tight lip about their business."

"You are right I found that out for myself today. The only other person I have to turn to now is Uncle Charles. I'm going to call him later today."

"Well good luck with that. He is her brother, there's but so much he's going to tell you."

"Uncle Charles usually tells me everything. I'm his favorite niece I shouldn't have any problem getting anything out of him."

"That was in the past and this is a more sensitive subject about his sister. He also may have been sworn to secrecy."

"We'll see how he reacts when talk to him. If he acts nervous then I'll know what's up from there. Ok enough about that. How did your sorry date go last night? Veronica asked grinning.

"It went," Lawrence responded. He could hear the excitement in her voice but there was no way he was about to tell her that last night he proposed to the very woman she despised. She already warned him about going on the date so telling her that Naomi now wears his ring would get him cursed out for real. She probably would take back half of her business from him.

"That's all. It doesn't sound like there was nothing exciting that went on last night at all. See there I told you, I told you. I knew that date wasn't worth going on."

"Yeah you did. Actually, both you and Chasity told me not to go. Had I only listened."

"Now you are losing me. What did actually happen last night?"

"I would rather tell you in person than tell you over the phone. I'm not like you I do love you enough to tell you than for you to find out through someone else."

"Oh, Lord something terrible happened. Is she pregnant?"

"No…she's not pregnant."

"You caught something. Lord you are dying! Oh, Lord it's too soon. He's too young Lord!"

"Shut up woman! It's not that either."

"Then man what is? I'm tired of guessing."

"I'm not telling you. You just have to wait until you get home."

"See now that's cold and dirty. Now when I get home and I see a baby bump I'm not buying not one damn diaper because you should've been honest the first time." Veronica had Lawrence thinking about that thing. Did he even wear a condom the night before? Boy that woman was really trying to get me! He thought.

"Well you can just block that out of your mind too (he hoped)."

"Well I see my dad finally coming out so I have to cut this convo short. I love you and we will continue this messiness later."

"I love you too. Please keep me up to date about mom and this mystery lady thing. And thanks for finally calling me back, nice to know that I was somewhere next Warren on your agenda."

"Ok will do. No problem and you're petty!"

"Anyway, tell dad I said hi and you better not have too much fun."

"Whatever, I promise to keep both legs raised just for you," Veronica stated laughing out loud.

"That was not funny Veronica dammit!"

"Yes, it was. Bye."

"BYE!"

Hee, hee, hee that was funny to me. "Who were you talking to Peaches. I could hear you laughing way in the parlor?"

"Daddy who else makes me laugh that hard."

"Lawrence! You tell him I said hello."

"No but he did say to tell you, mom and precious Val hi."

"So, Peaches are you enjoying any of this vacation so far?"

"Hmm." They both burst out laughing. At least my dad does have my sense of humor she thought. "I'm not quite sure how to answer that just yet. It's still early."

"I understand. Some weird things have happened in the past twenty-four hours."

"Care to elaborate?"

"Baby girl there's nothing to elaborate on. All I know is I see that this vacation was very much needed for all of us. It shows that we all are so much out of touch and it's pathetic. Not one of us get along at all. That for me is a hard pill to swallow. I don't know what's going on with anyone especially your mom."

"Really dad? I beg to differ."

"Peaches you say that like you have something to ask me."

"Dad I asked you questions earlier and you shut me down. Like always this family is full of secrets no one honestly tell anyone anything."

"Well Peaches all I can say is what being done in the dark will one day come to the light. It's just that now is not the time to talk about it. When we feel, the time is right we will."

"I guess I have to take that huh?" (yeah for now until I get home or talk to Uncle Charles).

"I wish you promise me that you would leave it for now."

"Yelp, ok… yeah, you said it."

"Ok now that's over with. Where's your mom and sister. I said one hour. If I have to go get them there's going to be some problems."

"Just give them a few more minutes I guess they should be here soon. While we wait what else is on the agenda for the day?"

"I had us signed up for horseback riding since we are in Texas as well as, some cattle ranching. Sounds fun, right?"

"Yea fun! Did you talk any of this over with your wife? You know how she and your daughter dresses. I just don't see either one of them doing those in their normal attire. Just in case you hadn't let me get my camera phone ready." Veronica laughed deviously.

"Great Peaches rub it in. Lord please help me with these women."

Right when he got that comment out of his mouth there walked up his wife and his daughter dressed in peach and white with matching sandals. Nobody chose to wear dark colors and nobody wore sneaker. Don't get me wrong they both were extremely beautiful. Their skin was so beautiful it was like they both had been kissed by the sun so it was obvious they went to the tanning booth. So, with them taking time out to look that incredible what Robert had in mind Veronica knew was completely out of the question. She already had her phone ready and recording from the time they hit the corner.

The look on her dad's face was priceless. I wouldn't miss recording that for the world she thought. "Hi everyone, Valerie gleamed. We finally made it back. We apologize for the wait. We both made a stop off at the spa before we came over. Can't you tell."

"Yes, Veronica chimed in, you both looked absolutely beautiful. Don't they dad?"

"Yes, they do Peaches, he answered trying to crack a smile."

"Well thank you Ronica! That was really sweet of you."

"Well handsome what's on the agenda for the remainder of the day?" Debra questioned softly kissing Richard on the lips."

"Yeah dad what's on the agenda for the REMAINDER of the evening?" Veronica asked with a chuckled.

"What's so funny Veronica?" Debra questioned irate.

"It's nothing baby. You know how Peaches can be. She likes having fun."

"Uh huh. Baby you neglected to answer my question."

Richard took a deep breath. Everything Veronica recently stated was rushing thorough his mind. "Well for starters…"

"Uh oh here it comes."

"Peaches please! Ok like I was saying before I was rudely interrupted. Well I signed us up for horseback riding since we are in Texas as well as, some cattle ranching, after that we will have dinner then either we can all do something together or we can all go our separate ways."

We all held our breathes. I waited for the ground to open and something evil to come sprouting out. But nothing. Mom's face turned beet red but she just reminded quiet with her hand rubbing her forehead for seemed like two hours. When she lifted her head up she had this weird grin on her face and simply said "Ok".

"Ok…" I almost took off running I just knew this woman's head was about to spin around. She sounds pleasant but that look on her face was saying something totally different.

"Like I said ok baby, whatever you say. If that what you want to do it's fine with me. I just wished you would've called and informed me of this before I decided to wear this but it's fine. I will make it work. I always do."

"Well mom you don't speak for me I am NOT about to get on nobody's horse with no white Capri's on. You can forget that."

"Yes, you are young lady, Debra stated walking slowly and very close up to Valerie's face. You are going and you're going to like it! You hear me!" Val's face turned beet red this time. It was almost like she had seen a crazy woman or her worst nightmare. If I hadn't' seen it for myself I wouldn't believe it. Ever since that woman appeared my mom has been acting very weird. Something is wrong and that woman has her by the strings.

"Ok ladies let's please go have some must needed fun. Please!"

"Yes please. I think I better walk way over here. Heck I think I will be ok walking in the middle of the street with the moving traffic!"

"You're forever trying to be funny. Get your ass in the car!" Debra ushered Veronica."

"Yes, ma'am don't chew my head off. You to Val. Are riding with me?"

"I think I better. Is it even safe for me to talk?"

Veronica burst out laughing before she knew it.

"It's not funny Ronica. What in the world is wrong with her. She's been acting bipolar all morning. One minute she's really sweet, the next she's about to bit my head off."

"Was she like this when you two were together?"

"Heck yes! Girl I was so afraid of her. It was so strange. To keep her from going off I just did everything she asked me to do. Poor dad I can only imagine the hell he's about to catch."

Veronica looked down at her phone. There was a missed text from Lawrence she paused before she read it. This was the first time her and Valerie had a real sister conversation in years she didn't want to interrupt it. She decided to open it anyway. It read:

"I see you didn't mention you passing out last night. Don't think I forgot. Oh, yeah don't think I didn't see you laying there with pretty boy holding your hand like you two supposedly be some kind of exclusive couple. Like I said before you better come back a virgin Ronica and I'm not playing around. You get there around him and act like you've lost your mind if you want to but you know what's up. ☺. Later!"

Oh no he didn't she thought! That negro has lost his mind for real. When did he think he could start telling me what to do? He doesn't boss me around, and he most defiantly does not tell me what to do with my body parts. He MOST DEFIANTLY does not tell me who to have sex with and who to give my body away to. I see it's a lot of things we should finally set straight. He has been crossing his boundaries a lot lately and it's my fault because I have been allowing him to.

"I see your mood has changed after reading that text. Who was that?"

"Nobody important, just something that I need to finally set straight that's all. So, what are we going to do about this mom thing? Did you get a chance to ask her any questions about last night."

"Are you kidding me? Heck no! I wouldn't dare ask her nothing not the way she's been acting. I wanted so bad to ask her about that woman from last night. I kinda think that lady called her today."

"Really why you say that?"

"While we were getting, our toes done, she was talking to this person on the phone. It sounded like a female's voice. The conversation was ok at first then it escalated to something serious towards the end. I didn't get the chance to see who it was she was talking to because by that time she had stepped out of the room. You could hear her arguing all the way where I was. You know how her voice escalates when she's upset."

"Yeah I do. I think you just experienced a little of that for yourself."

"Whatever. All I know who ever it was is the cause for mom's sudden mood swings."

"Now that I can believe."

"Ronica if I tell you something will you believe me."

"Which part? You suppose to have a secret or the fact that you want to share it with me?"

"Funny…, Valerie squinted her eyes at Veronica. No seriously I have some news."

"Is it supposed to be a secret?"

"For now, yeah."

"Ok shoot. I promise to keep it to myself."

"Ok you promise."

"Girl yes! I said I would geesh!"

"Ok, Valerie answered grinning. I met someone."

"....."

"What Ronica?"

"Girl what the hell is so secretive about that?"

"I'm saying he's not someone you would expect me to be with. You actually already met him."

"Try me."

"You're not even going to guess who it is?"

"Nope."

"Come on Ronica! Please."

"Nope, just tell me."

"Ok…It's AARON!"

"OOH yea!!!!"

"Aw come on you can't say you already knew it was him?"

"Um yeah I did. When we were leaving earlier I seen you two kissing in the parking lot."

"NO! You did?"

"Yeah, lucky for you dad had his back turnt and was getting into the car."

"Oh, my God waiting until I tell him this!"

"So, when did this happen?"

"Yesterday at when we came down to meet Warren. He introduced himself as I was leaving."

"Ok I'm confused. You said that Warren asked you out yesterday."

"Well he did, and so did Aaron. I accepted Aaron's proposal first."

"Really Val?"

"We're not back on this are we Ronica? We were doing good without bring up his name. We are not going to be those type of sisters. Please!"

"Whatever Val." Veronica chose to let it go for now anyway. There was no need to keep pressing the issue. It's seemed that Valerie has finally moved on anyway. She was now ready to spend some quality time with Warren now anyway. Her dad did mention that they had some free time later. So, she was thinking that she would spend that free time with him.

"Is he a nice guy?"

"So far yes. I enjoy his company. He makes me laugh and he's fun to be around."

"I say keep seeing him. You never know what could happen. Besides you're getting old you can't afford to keep throwing too many back."

"Aww now there you go. Valerie smiled, and thanks. Like said I like him, and you never know he could one day be the one."

"Yeah, he might be. The best thing about it is taking the time to find out."

"That is true. I really like him Ronica. He's so cool. Far different from any man I have dated in the past."

"I've noticed," Veronica responded. Her mind couldn't help but travel back to the scene she walked up on this morning. The scene of Mr. Muscle as her dad calls him; fondling on Valerie and her mom. She just hoped that him touching both her and her mother doesn't turn out to be pattern with him. He could turn out to be the type of man that don't know how to keep his hands to himself.

*　*　*

The Martin Family enjoyed their time out together. They all haven't laughed at each other and together like that in years. It was funny watching their mom Debra trying to straddle a horse in sandals while trying to keep her whites clean. She did very well despite not being on a horse in a while. Valerie spent her time trying to ride cute and flirting with the rancher. I tell you that girl really knows how to milk being a model for everything that it's worth.

I can't remember the last time I've seen my dad laugh and smile so much. On top of that mean it. That man showed his behind off.

I hadn't realized how physical fit he was still even at his age. He was riding horses and taming the animals better than the ranchers half his age. My favorite part was feeding the animals of course. I haven't been on a ranch in years so just like the others I weren't too excited about going. But when I got there I was ok being around the cattle and the other animals. Especial the baby rabbits and ducks. But… the later it gotten the more I was like ok this is enough. We had been there since about eleven thirty. It was now two thirty. Not only was I starving I still haven't seen Warren play not one round of golf today. I haven't heard from him since this morning. I'm sure by now he must think that I'm not coming. I tried sneaking to check the score several times, but my dad was watching us like hawks.

Every time me or Val touched our phones he was like "Nope, no phones. This is our family time. No phones today ladies. Those guys and your friends can wait until later."

I don't know what this trip has done to him but I'm not use to him being so bossy. I'm used to him being more laid back and being the whatever goes type. But not this trip. He's been more of a bull dog. I'm not sure who mom brought with her but I'm about to think she needs to send this one back and bring back our real dad!

I walked around the front of the stables to see where everyone has gotten to. Valerie was over in the corner of course with one of the handsome stable guys. In her defense she had to do something to help her pass time. I've seen mom and dad walking up the path holding hands. They seemed to be getting along fairly well today. This place may have something to do with it. It was a beautiful setting. You couldn't help but fall in love.

After a minute a realized that I was the only one standing there alone. It went from looking beautiful to feeling rather awkward. I know for sure I was ready to go now.

I was ready to get out of these clothes and put on something sexy then head over to Warren's later. It looked like I weren't going to catch any of his round today due to family time. It's disappointing but it's something I may have to accept. I'm sure he's going to be upset that he didn't get to see me but I pray he don't be that upset.

"Well ladies, yawl about ready," called out Richard.

"Mm looked who's been in Texas for two days and trying to pick the accent," laughed Debra.

"It's addictive."

"I know that's right. Just the way of life around here period is addictive. Richard? Ever thought about moving here?"

"I don't know baby Houston is a beautiful place to live. It's something to think about."

"I wouldn't be upset if you did. I would give me a reason to visit, "Valerie stated smiling at the handsome stable guy."

"Well it doesn't really matter to me. I don't have a reason to come here but it's a delightful place to visit."

"As usual she's in brat form."

"Cut it out you two," Debra warned. We haven't set anything in stone it was just a thought"

"Yes, so don't go causing a fight over nothing."

"Fine. All I was saying is that I don't have any friends or anything here that's all."

"Neither does either of us, but there's nothing wrong with meeting new people."

"I guess so."

"So, anybody hungry! I know I am. It's now almost four p.m. Let's say we head back to our rooms rest up, get dressed and meet each other at the restaurant no later than 6:30 Valerie for your birthday celebration!" proclaimed Richard.

"Why are you directing everything towards me I'm not always the one running late."

Everyone looked at each other. **Yes, you are,**" they all said in unison.

"Whatever, Valerie said rolling her eyes, watch I beat everyone there. You'll see."

"I think we need to put a wager on that one. I see everyone $20."

"Put us down for $20 each," Debra stated.

"I see I'm going to be $60 richer for my birthday because all of you are going to lose your money this time. Watch! Just watch!"

"Sure! Thanks, you for the free meal," Veronica laughed.

"Whatever heffa."

"Ok ladies let's go. Debra and I will see you Veronica around 6:30. We'll see you Val round 7:45 ish."

"I'm hurt dad that you have no faith in me."

"I do pudding it's just that I know my baby girl," Richard stated kissing her on the forehead.

"Yeah, yeah."

Veronica drove back to their rooms as quick as she could. She managed to make it through the very heavy traffic and drop Valerie off to her car. All of this before 4:25. She wanted to make sure she had enough time to lay across her bed for a minute, after all she had been up since 6:30 that morning. She was now extremely tired and needed at least a twenty-minute nap before she did anything else.

Before she could lay down she received a text from Warren asking if she still coming to the country club. She started to text him back but she didn't know what to say. She knew if she said no that would disappoint him. She also knew there was no chance she could get dressed and be there before his round ended either. So, either way it was going to disappoint him. So, she did the next best thing and didn't respond at all. She chose to answer him back later, hoping she would remember before it gets too late.

She set her timer 4:50 to make sure she has enough time to get dressed and be to the restaurant on time. The alarm went off on time but Veronica kept pressing the snooze button. Before she knew it, the time was now 5:15. She jumped up out of bed before she knew it. She almost gave herself a heart attack she jumped up so fast.

She realized that she was running out of time so she quickly picked out something to wear, plugged in her curing iron and turned her shower on. She heard some humming coming from the living room. She peeped her head in to see what nobody but Val was up to. "What are you doing?"

"Resting. What are you doing?" Like always Valerie looked like she jumped off the cover of a magazine. Before she came to the room she stopped off at the spa had her make done and her hair curled. Why in the hell didn't I think of that? "Why didn't you tell me you were stopping off at the spa?"

"Oh, I didn't think that was your thing. Me and mom stopped by and had everything done before we came up. We made our appointments this morning. You better hurry up and get ready sugar. Times a wasting. And it looks like you're going to need a lot of it. I would get right on that if I were you."

Veronica looked at her sister bit on her lips, screamed and stomped back to her room slamming the door extra hard. Valerie just laughed and continued reading her magazine and sipping on her tea. Veronica spent the remainder of her time going back and forth like mad woman trying her best to be dressed on time and look as equally gorgeous as her mom and sister will look tonight.

She hated them both she wanted to scream but she knew she had to get herself together. She managed to finish on time but not a moment too soon. She had to admit she pulled it off no thanks to her siblings. She did manage to look flawless she may add. She opts on a short gold mini with matching stilettos. She kept her hair bone straight to save time and her makeup was beautifully natural. Yes, she was lovely she thought.

She stepped out to see her lovely sister draped in an orange flowing off the shoulders short dress with gold matching heels. Her hair lovely pulled to the side and was wearing a birthday tiara from earlier. She looked absolutely gorgeous as always. I say we all should deduct $10 for cheating, after all she did go to the spa.

We both get to the restaurant on the time. We were greeted by my dad who was all smiles and somewhat in disbelief. He couldn't believe his eyes. Me and Valerie actually showed up together. He was glad to see that she took the initiative and put the family first by not making it seem like we were on her time. He hugged the both of us and showed us to our table.

Mom was already seated and waiting for us. She looked just as lovely as us both. She's worn all white and gold. She had a long white off the shoulders flowy dress and gold heels. I not sure why they both chose to dress alike, but whatever. We hadn't all planned wearing gold but I loved the fact that we all shared the same mind. My dad had on an off white fitted suit that I had to say made him look both handsome and young.

We all sat down and had a wonderful diner. Something we haven't done in a very long time. The atmosphere was even different that evening. Something Veronica hadn't experienced since they were kids. Everything just felt right. Her and Valerie was getting along. Her parents were getting along, they were even acting like they loved one another. "Ok birthday girl make a wish," Debra sang excitedly. We got Valerie her favorite color cake. It was orange and cream butter cream filled three tier princess cake the same color she was wearing. It was a beautiful cake but like Val a bit over the top. We all sang happy birthday to her that made her feel super special.

"So, how does it feel to be drawing social security Val, asked Veronica"

"Hold it! I'm only turning twenty-nine! I'm not even thirty yet."

"Forget that when am I going to start seeing some grand babies running around here from the both of you."

"Mom I'm working on it, "Valerie responded rolling her eyes. Veronica never said a word everyone knew she was still a virgin. There was no way she would have an honest believable response for any of them.

"Ronica?"

"Um… Piece of cake anyone?"

"Now that's what I wanted to hear," boasted Richard.

"Richard that WOMAN is now be almost twenty-seven years old at the end of the year. She can't stay a virgin forever."

"She's still my baby I say yes she can."

"Oh Lord!" Veronica sighed. Not this again. Someone please change the subject she prayed.

"Ok pay up," Valerie extended out her hand.

"What?"

"You all heard me. I want my money."

"Nope. First of all she had help dad."

"What? What kind of help?"

"Both her and mom stopped off at the spa before they dressed. On top of that they didn't even ask me if I wanted to go. I say deduct $10 each."

"No, no, Ms. Petty Boots. I earned my money fair and square. It's not my fault you didn't think of it first that's what this is all about. I want my money."

"That's right. Veronica stated laughing. I was pissed had me running around everywhere like a mad women. While you're sitting in the living room sipping tea. I was so pissed off at her."

"I could imagine. I would be too," Debra stated laughing.

"I started to snatched those curls out of her head I was so mad."

"I bet you were," snapped Valerie.

"Oh let it go," Debra pleased.

"Yes Val I was only kidding hun."

"Anyway. Did anyone get to see any of the round today? Veronica? I know Warren finished with eight under par. He's currently in 3rd place. They said he shot a very good round today."

Oh shoot! She thought. I had forgotten to text him back. I know he's pissed with me. It would be in poor taste to text him back now. God! How in the world did I forget to do something stupid like that? It's now nine thirty. Dang it! I have to call him for sure tomorrow and apologize.

"You're quiet Veronica. Is everything ok."

"Honestly no, but it will be."

"Anything we can do to help, "questioned Richard.

"No daddy, I have to take care of this problem myself but thanks for the offer."

"Ok Peaches, you know I'm here if you need me."

"Yeah I know daddy."

"So are we Ronica," chimed in her mom and Valerie.

She had to pause for a second on that one but managed to get out "Ok...thanks."

Around 10:30 they all finished their dinner and went their separate ways for evening. Valerie lied and claimed she was going to turn in for the evening, but she didn't know Veronica over heard her making plans to meet old Aaron later. Apparently she were to meet up with him for a night cap. So you know what that meant. Eww nasty!

I'm not sure what mom and dad had planned not that I cared or even want to know. Once again, she was alone with nothing to do and no one to talk to. She had all but blew Warren off early so she knew there was no chance of getting with him. She could head out somewhere and find something to get into She reasoned. I am looking way too cute to go back to the room this early.

As Veronica was headed up the stairs to retrieve her car she bumps into the last person she would think would be there.

CHAPTER 10

And the Bomb Drops!

On her way, out the door Veronica heads up stairs to retrieve her car from the Valet. While going up the steps she had her head down searching through her purse for her number. She bumped into a lady she and managed to get excuse me out but the lady was very rude about it. She looked up see what all the commotion about. When she looked up not only was it the lady from yesterday that was rude to her but she was with Warren. She knew they weren't dating or anything but she was still surprised to see him there with that woman.

"Well, hi Warren," Veronica spoke confused.

"Hi. Veronica, right?"

Wow! So, now he's trying to act like he doesn't know who I am. Ok, he wants to play that game. I guess he is pissed.

"Yes, it is. Ms. Martin actually."

"Yeah right…I didn't see you on the greens today Ms. Martin."

"I was busy. You know doing family things. VACATION things you know how that can be."

"I can imagine. I did pretty good today. Did you happen to see any of the score today?"

"Nope, can't say I did. You know being busy and all."

"Mm. I see. By the way this is a CLOSE friend of mine Angela. Angela this is Ms. Martin. You remember I told you about her father the owner of Martin's A Set Above Golf Apparel."

"Oh yeah, now I remember. Nice to meet the persons that will be creating my baby's future golf attire."

"Really now?"

"Well that's what I was told right honey. At least that's what he said when I've seen your number appear on his phone earlier."

"Oh really! Well Mr. Beasley I look forward to working with you and my dad ONLY in the future."

"I guess so."

"Well let me go and let you two finish enjoying your evening. Will talk to you another time Mr. Beasley. Good-bye now."

Veronica walked off as quickly as she could. Her hands were sweating so bad this time she could barely hold her keys. She doesn't know if it was from the embarrassment or anger. The nerve of him! Like always the female was standing there doing all the talking and he had nothing to say. She stood outside waiting for her car when she received a text.

"Veronica, I apologize about what just happened. I know it looked bad. I was just upset about you standing me up earlier. Can I please see you later and make all of this up to you? Please call me back later. If not I'll call you. Just don't stop talking to me over this. Please except my apology. ☹."

Veronica turns her phone the hell off. She had enough of men and their nonsense over the years. Everyone was constantly asking her why was she still single. It was because of men like that that's why. She was madly in love with this guy named Reggie she had met right after college once. He was a NFL player out of Cleveland. He was the tallest and the smoothest man she had ever seen before in her life. Other than Lawrence of course.

The only problem with him was that he was way too much into himself and he was too clingy. He demanded too much of her time and since they lived in two different states it was hard to keep up with one another.

She was still very much in love with him but just not a fan of long distant relationships. At least he was honest and not full of bull. Now the fact that he was way too into himself was another story. I'm beginning to think that I'm attracted to men like Lawrence all the way around. I guess that was my down fall she was thinking. If I could stay away from men like him I would be alright.

What Mr. Beasley had just done he can keep all that to himself. I can tell he don't know nothing about me she thought. I don't do jealousy. He has the wrong female. I am way too strong for that. Well, I guess I'll head downtown to check out the scenery and see what's popping. I may check the nearest bar since I'm alone in a new town I don't want to go too far being by myself.

Veronica turned her phone back on after thirty minutes had passed. She was thinking that was long enough for Warren to get the hint. Her phone buzzed when she pulled off. Yes! She yelled it was the call she had been waiting for. Her Uncle Charles finally called her back after all day. She prays he had the answers to all the questions she had going on in her mind.

"Hi Uncle Charles! How have you been?"

"Hi there my Georgia Peach! I am doing wonderful baby girl. How's the family?"

"We are all doing great."

"I can tell you're still alive and not in jail. I take the family vacation is going well?"

"Yes, sir it is. As hard it is to believe."

"How's that smooth ass brother in-law of mine?"

"He's doing well Uncle Charles," Veronica answered laughing.

"And my crazy as… I meant my lovely sister?"

"Ha! You are funny Unk but she's fine."

"So, my Georgia Peach what's up. Why you've been trying to get in touch with me so much here lately?"

"Well Unk, I have some questions but I don't know how to ask them."

"Well baby the best way to ask is to just to come right out with it."

"Ok. Unk, are you familiar with a woman by the name of Marylyn?"

The phone was eerily quiet on the other end. She couldn't understand why her uncle became so quiet suddenly. It was like she had mentioned a ghost. "Unk? Are you still there?"

"Yeah I'm still here. What made you ask me about Marylyn of all people?"

"So, you have heard of her?"

"Yes I have. My question is how do you know her?"

"Well Unk she was spotted at the fundraiser last night. Valerie even witnessed her and mom getting into a fist fight after everything was over. I've over heard her mom and dad getting into a heated argument over something myself. All I kept hearing her ask repeatedly "Why didn't you tell her". All I was saying was tell who what? When I asked dad he just brushed the whole ordeal off and pretty much told me to stop asking questions."

"Anything else he had to tell you?"

"Yeah he said what's in the dark will one day come to the light."

"Well there you have it. I'm sorry to say that I'm not at liberty to say no more than what he told you. My lips are sealed."

"You can't tell me anything?"

"Sorry my Georgia Peach I've said way too much already. I have to go."

"But Unk!"

"Bye baby girl." Well dang he acts as if our call was being recorded he got off so fast! Something is going on and I'm going to get down to the bottom of it.

*   *   *

Chasity was glad to finally be back home. She felt like she's been gone for a month instead of only one week. The first thing she did was checked her mail and tied up all her other loosed ends she left undone. The main loose end she had to tackle was finally getting the issue with Lawrence out of her system. She decided today was the day that she would finally tell him what she had on her mind.

She had met a wonderful man named Chad. Not only was he handsome but he was rich and he was madly in love with her. She had to admit she was falling for him as well. It was time to put Lawrence out of her system and put their false romance behind her once and for all.

She finished running her errands and went home to get dressed. She wanted to throw on the sexiest outfit she could find in her closet. She remembered she had a sexy black and white fitted dress hanging up in her closet that she never worn. It was eighty degrees out today so high heeled strapped sandals would be perfect. A light Smokey eye and a soft red lip with her hair softly pulled up will set off the whole look. She showered and threw on his favorite scent Warm Vanilla. He was the type that like women scented but nothing too over the top. She gave herself one more look over in the mirror. She knew she was fine. She smiled and walked out the door.

Chasity pulled up to boutique but was too afraid to get out. Like before she chickened out when it was time to finally confront him. She decided to call ahead to make sure he was there. She didn't want to drive way down there just to get there and he's nowhere to be found. Like always it went straight to voice mail. Shoot! She thought, maybe he's not there. Then again, it's only two thirty in the afternoon he could be in a business meeting.

She decided to take a chance anyway. She had been sitting on this long enough. Hopefully he hadn't eaten that way she could treat him out to lunch. Maybe he wouldn't be too upset if she told him over a full stomach. She finally muscled up enough nerve to get out of the car and walk into the building.

Their cute receptionist Melissa was sitting at the front and greeted her with a huge smile. "Welcome Ms. Simms! You look lovely as always. How may I help you today? Ms. Martin is currently still out of town but Mr. Weldon is here." I loved this girl, she talked way too much. She always told me what I wanted to know before I even asked her a thing.

"Hi hunni bun. You look lovely yourself as usual. Could you please send Mr. Weldon a message and let him know that I'm here?"

"Sure, just give me one minute," she offered with a smile.

Chasity waited for a moment for his response. Hopefully it won't take him too long to get back with her. "Ms. Simms, he said for you to have a seat and that he'll be right with you. While you wait could I get you anything?"

"No honey, I'm good. You've are done good already."

"Thank you, ma'am, just let me know if you need anything in the process while you wait."

"Ok thanks." Chasity felt herself getting nervous all over again. "Ok girl she said to herself. This is the day. It's either now or never." While she was seated, she seen huge breast Naomi come walking to the front looking like a bomb shell in a bad light blue knee length dress. She had her hair bone straight, with matching light blue heels on. I tell you the chick was bad but why the hell was she up here instead of Lawrence? Nobody called for her.

"Hi Chasity," Naomi greeted her with a fake smile.

"Stop the fake pleasantry. Why are you here?"

"I was sent here because my man is busy. So… what is it I can help you with?"

"Your man! Excuse me heffa?"

"Um you're not about to get loud in here, but yes my man I'm his fiancé'," Naomi stated showing Chasity a very huge ring. Chasity nearly fell out of her seat. Not because of the size of the ring, it was that she couldn't believe her eyes and ears. Was she being punked? By now she wobbly stood to her feet with her fists balled up.

She felt her pass coming back to surface. She thought she had put her violent pass behind her but everything was slowly coming back to her. Naomi looked down and seen Chasity hands and slowly started to back away. By that time, Lawrence came floating around the corner. That man was so handsome everything he worn made him look he like he was modeling for a center fold. He had a concerned look on his face when he had seen them both standing there together.

When Lawrence walked up he was all smiles. He didn't think that Naomi would be that messy and tell Chasity about the ring right there at his job. "What's up Chasity! I just got the message that you were here. How have you been?"

"Hey baby I just told her the good news."

"What good news," he asked closing his eyes.

"I told her about my huge ring see," Naomi stated extending her hand in front of Chasity's face.

"Aww damn! Chasity baby can I talk to you for a minute?"

"Baby! No, you didn't just call her baby. First it was Veronica now her. Lawrence your ass has some explaining to do!"

"Look I think you've already said enough. Please go back in the conference room."

"I'm not going anywhere. What you have to say to her you're going to say right in front of me."

"Dammit woman! Chasity? Please just come outside with me for a minute."

Chasity just stood there looking at him with her temper fuming and hot tears running down her face. "So, all these years that's all I mean to you. You had to send your hoe out to tell me about your so-called engagement."

"It wasn't meant to happen like that baby. Please just let me explain."

"No, Lawrence. You had your chance. I hope her huge ass makes you happy."

"Oh, I will."

"Look, I didn't ask you nothing," Chasity screamed charging at Naomi.

"Ladies please!" pleaded Lawrence.

Chasity looked at Lawrence with repulsion and stormed outside. She couldn't dial Veronica's number fast enough. "Hello," she heard a pleasant voice on the other end.

"Hello, stated Chasity trying to fight back tears. Veronica…."

"Chasity? Baby what's wrong? Talk to me please!"

"I can't take it." was all she could get out.

"You can't take what? What is it? Tell me? Do I need to come home early?"

"Lawrence… Lawrence is engaged to Naomi! She screamed in the phone now in tears.

"WHAT! He's engaged to who! Are you kidding me." Veronica now understood the tears and the distance between her and her friend. She didn't need her to go into details about anything. Her tears over the situation alone let her know what was going on. "Where is he now?"

"Veronica who cares. I hate his guts. I don't ever want to say anything to him ever again."

"Well find him. I want to talk to the bastard!"

"Ok…" Chasity was now crying uncontrollably.

Chasity didn't have to look far. When she turned around Lawrence was standing right behind her. Apparently, he had followed her out the door. "Here Veronica wants to talk to you."

"Aw damn! Really? I'm not in the mood to talk to that woman right now.

"Take the PHONE!"

"Ok! God! Hello!"

"Don't get loud with me. When were you planning on telling us this news? Or was this the so-called secret you were planning on tell me yesterday?"

"Ronica, it's not like I weren't going to tell you it's just that I didn't know how to tell you."

"You know she has to go right? There's no way she can work there and be engaged to you. It's against policy."

"C'mon Ronica don't do this to her."

"I'm not doing it to her you are. I told you not to mess around with her at the beginning but did you listen, like always no. You did like you normally does and listen with your penis. And don't tell me you didn't notice that Chasity was in love with you."

"You saying you did."

"Lawrence yes, for a long time. You would have to be naïve not to. Then again, I forgotten who I was talking to. You have to fix this mess, and it better be fixed before I get back."

"So, the only way Naomi don't lose her job is if we are both married correct?"

"Boy don't tell me you're going to do something stupid?"

"Just answer my question."

"Lawrence it's your funeral. Just let me know where to send the flowers."

"You told me to handle it and that's what I'm going to do. It's time that I clean up my own mess."

"Get off my phone man!"

"Love you too Ronica."

"Put Chaz back on the phone."

Lawrence walked over and gave the phone back to Chasity. She wouldn't even look up at him. "Hey hunni bunny. I don't know what to tell you but that you're going to be alright and we're to get through this together. I'm here with you through this and you can call me every five minutes if you need to until you get over it. Now you do know we have to talk about you keeping this from me at some point." Veronica demanded.

"Yeah I know. I love you for sticking by me despite my attitude and all of my pettiness."

"Love you too, I'll be home soon and we can talk about it more than. Besides I have a lot to tell you! On top that I may need your help with investigating something."

"Ok sure thing. Love you talk to you soon."

"Love you too. Bye."

"Bye."

Just then Chasity sees a familiar car pull up. It was Chad. She was confused about why he was there. She hadn't remembered telling him where she lived nor where Veronica worked at that. He looked incredibly handsome getting out of that gold colored Beamer. He was unusually dressed down today. He wore a white printed t-shirt with matching Nikes with dark colored jeans with a matching jacket. His hair was curly and he looked like he was just fresh from the barber.

The site of him made her feel a lot better about the Lawrence situation. Before she could run to hug him that's when she seen Naomi running towards him. She grabbed him and kisses him on the cheek.

"Hey baby! Naomi grabbed him excitedly. You finally made it."

Baby! I see somebody is about to die today! Chasity screamed angrily.

EPILOGUE

The week for the Martins was finally almost over. They had all survived it without killing one another. Veronica's dad did get a chance to see the final round of the tournament, but without her of course. She made up a simple lie and just said that she was tired from all the excitement from the weekend to attend. There was no way she was about to show her face after what transpired that evening.

She was glad to hear that Warren managed to win the tournament. Richard stated that he finished with -10 under par. I've seen on television and pictures that Ms. Angela was all over his arm after he won. That's typical. I was upset because that could've been me but that was another story within itself.

We enjoyed the remainder of our time together as a family site seeing, attending concerts, shopping, spending time at the spa and eating out way too much. I think we all gained at least five pounds each. Including the Diva Val herself.

It has been two years since we've enjoyed each other's company like this. At the beginning, I honestly didn't see none of this happening. I complicated not even showing up. You know what? I must say I am glad I came.

Our family had just come back from seeing an exhibit at one of the largest aquariums in Houston. Apparently, my family are a bunch of lushes because we all wanted to go out for drinks. My mom and I relationship must be getting better because she's starting to ask me to do things. Not like I missed that part growing up but I rather do that instead of arguing. Mom had forgotten her id so she asked me to retrieve it for her. That was an unusual request because it was not like her to send me to do anything that was Val's job.

She stated that the id should be in her top drawer beside the bed on the left-hand side. Like always nothing was ever where your parents said it was. Veronica looked where she said it should be and the id wasn't there. So, she looked in the top drawer on the opposite side of the room. Just as she thought there it was. She also seen something else hidden in the drawer as well. It was a folder with pictures in it.

It wasn't like she was trying to purposely be noisy. She gasped when she opened the folder. There were pictures of her mom and that Marylyn lady from birth all the way to adulthood. She flipped the baby photo over and it read: Mommy's beautiful twins Denise and Debra Thompson Jan 5, 1963. Mequon, WI. That…mystery… woman…is…my…mother's twin sister! That lady dad was kissing is my AUNT! What in the world is going on around here? Her name is not even Marylyn it's Denise! Veronica's head was now as light as a feather. How could that be? Mom said she didn't have any sisters. The only sibling, she claims is Uncle Charles. That still doesn't explain why Uncle Charles was so hush, hush a few nights ago.

Just then Veronica heard the door open and her mom called out her name. She nearly peed herself she was so scared. She couldn't get those pictures back in the folder fast enough. She took the baby picture and stuffed it down her bra and closed the drawer. She hurried to the side of her mother's bed but not a moment too soon. Her mother had just peeped her head in the bedroom. "Hey there you are! Girl didn't you hear me calling you? What were you doing up here so long?" Once again Veronica was speechless. This time she was sure it was out of fear!

My twin baby girls Denise and Debra? Why did her mother chose to keep her aunt of all people a secret? Why would she continue to lie about her existence? That still doesn't explain why her dad Richard was kissing her. It wasn't like he was confused. They both had different colored hair. One thing Veronica just remembered they both had sandy colored hair in the picture. That means her mother must have colored her hair at some point over the years. That would explain why she always seen color laying in the bathroom and kitchen growing up.

Either way someone was going to finally give her some answers. Rather it be ma Debra or her new found Aunt Marylyn/Denise!